DIGITAL WALLS

A CYBERPUNK SAGA

MATTHEW A. GOODWIN

DIGITAL WALLS

A Cyberpunk Saga
Book 3
MATTHEW A. GOODWIN

Independently published via KDP

ISBN Number 978-1-7340692-0-4

Editor: Bookhelpline.com

Cover design by Christian Bentulan

For my fellow drudges.
You know who you are.
I couldn't have done this without you.

PART I

CHAPTER 1

M oss opened his eyes, the smell of the sea filling his nose. He leaned forward, confused, and looked around his hex.

He was home.

He felt his body, running his hands over his torso. No wounds, nothing.

He didn't understand.

He heard a distant, tinny voice from what he assumed was the speaker mounted to the wall. "We have to keep him alive."

He looked up to the speaker. The woman's voice was just out of reach. He blinked hard, trying to make sense of it.

The last thing he remembered was being shot in Carcer City.

"Let him die and we'll just extract his chip," he heard someone say. The voice was familiar. He recognized it but couldn't quite place it.

The woman spoke again. "ThutoCo doesn't want competitors stealing proprietary information. He dies, the chip will self-destruct. It is why we've been working on him first."

"We brought him here so the techs could access the data,"

the familiar voice said. "If you are telling me you can't do it, we will find someone who can."

"I'm not saying that. I'm simply saying it's complicated and will take time," the woman said, sounding combative.

"Time is not a luxury either of us have," the familiar voice responded. Moss leaned forward toward the speaker, focusing and trying to place the voice.

He looked around his hex and stood, more confused than he had ever been. He didn't understand how he was home or how he was hearing the voices. He didn't even believe he was alive.

"We will work on this around the clock," Moss heard before silence descended.

"Kiddo," he heard and looked up.

Moss's eyes went wide. "Dad?"

His father rushed over and hugged him. "You're back!" His father sounded delighted.

"Back in the program?" Moss asked, knowing his father was dead and that the program containing the AI construct of his dad had been destroyed.

He rubbed his implant at the base of his skull.

His father took that as a sign to move away. "Did you do it?"

Moss blinked hard and shook his head, trying to understand. "Where are we?"

"In the program I designed," his father put plainly, looking perplexed.

"But we are in my hex now and. . ." he paused. "And the program was destroyed."

"Oh," his dad said, stroking his chin thoughtfully. His face turned grim. "Oh," he repeated.

"What?" Moss demanded.

His father shifted nervously, avoiding eye contact. Moss had forgotten just how lifelike this virtual version of his father was. It had been mapped on his personality using technology which he had created and it was a near-perfect replica.

"What?" Moss asked again, taking a softer tone. He was anxious and wanted to know what his father had figured out.

"When your mother worked the encryption," he began, looking disappointed. "I think she may have added more."

Moss felt his heart race. Even in a digital recreation, his body responded. "That's right! Grandma said there was more to this program than I knew."

His father looked at him with shock. "You, you spoke to my mother?"

Moss looked at his dad. He was wearing a look of over-whelmed confusion.

"Yes," Moss told him. "A lot has happened since we spoke."

"Seems that way," his father said. "Can you tell me about it? Do you have time?"

Moss looked around. "I think I do. I'm pretty sure this is a dream. Or I'm running the program in my sleep."

"Where are you?"

Moss looked at his father and gestured for him to take a seat in the small kitchen area. They sat and Moss told him what had happened. He explained that they had successfully infiltrated ThutoCo and prevented the company from killing the employees. Moss told him about Carcer and how Grimy had betrayed them and they ended up in Carcer City. His father wept as Moss told him that his mother had been captured and tortured, but they had got her out. His face grew more forlorn as Moss explained that he had been captured by Carcer in the process.

"So, you are in Carcer City?" his dad asked.

"I think so," Moss said, shrugging.

"If you are running my program, perhaps you can wake yourself up?" his dad offered.

Moss shook his head. "I don't think I can."

He looked at his father and smiled. He knew he was likely doomed. Figured his body would die in a holding cell as they hacked his implant. If he had to die, he was happy it would be with his family; digital or not.

"I'm so sorry for all you've been through," his dad said softly.

Moss could tell that he blamed himself. "Dad, it's not your fault. It's not anyone's fault. I've done some genuine good in the world. That has to count for something."

"It does," his father said, smiling with a parent's pride.

"Wait," Moss said as an idea occurred to him. "If you *are* the program, is there any way for you to run a diagnostic? Could you find out what you are capable of?"

His father cocked his head. "I suppose."

"Try," Moss urged. "Maybe we can figure something out."

His father smiled. "You really are something, kiddo. I always knew you were special, but you truly never cease to amaze me."

"I've had a lot of good teachers," Moss said, though he knew there was more to it than that. He had come to understand that he had good instincts, some capability deep within himself that he was only beginning to understand.

"Here I go," his father said, and his eyes went black.

Moss sat in silence, trying to listen for the voices from the speakers but hearing nothing. He wondered what was happening to his body and how much time was passing in the real world as he sat in this digital dream.

After a while, his father returned, blinking the black away and looking at his son. "There is a lot there."

"What does that mean?" Moss pressed.

"I'm not entirely sure," his dad admitted. "Frankly, I don't understand most of this stuff, but there seem to be remote controls, hacking software, and communication options. It's all Greek to me, but I tried to figure it out for you."

"Communication?" Moss asked excitedly.

"Looked that way. I could tell they were trying to make it simple on the back end so you could work it, but I don't know."

Moss stood and moved over to his work chair, the place where he had controlled his drudge in what felt like a previous life. A screen appeared and his father walked over to watch over his shoulder.

The program was hardwired to his brain, and he didn't need to use his hands to control the screen. His father had been right: He was met with a simple layout of options. There were words that he didn't fully understand and options he didn't recognize, but "communication" was clear.

He brought up the menu and thought about who he wanted to reach. Lines of code appeared, streaming downward in a shower of letters and symbols.

A long time passed as sweat beaded on Moss's forehead. He laughed to himself that the program was so unnecessarily real.

The screen crackled and went black before a blurry image of two calendars protruding from a face appeared.

"Moss?" Seti's voice transmitted, the mouth moving slowly after the words. "Is that you, are you all right?"

Moss had never been so happy to be talking with his team's eye in the sky. "Seti!" he exclaimed. "It's so great to hear a familiar voice!"

"Moss, how is this possible?" she asked, surprise clear in every word. "The layers of encryption, the networks you used to reach me, there is no way you did this yourself."

"It's a long story. Did the others make it out?" he asked. He knew he probably didn't have long to speak, but he needed to know how his friends were—how his grandmother was.

"They're fine, but Moss, this signal is weak," she warned.

"Seti, I'm alive and in Carcer City. Somehow, I'm using the program my parents constructed to contact you. If I can manage to wake up and get myself out, are there teams who can get to me?" Moss could hear the franticness in his voice.

He had no idea how he would wake his body up and even less of an idea of how he would escape if he did, but he needed to know if there was any hope.

"You may be alive, but you are not in C City," Seti told him.

His heart sank. "Where am I?"

"At one of Carcer's operational facilities," Seti's voice was strained and sad. "In Africa."

"What?" Moss and his father exclaimed in unison.

"I don't have any teams who can reach you quickly, and Detritus 16 have problems of their own and aren't answering my calls. I have a free agent who can get to you, but they wouldn't be able to break into where you are. I'll establish a secure network between you, but you'll need to get out if you have any hope of."

The screen went black.

"What the fuck is going on down here?" he heard the familiar man's voice come through the speaker.

Moss placed the voice. He couldn't believe it had taken him that long.

It was Warden Ninety-Nine: the man who had shot Ynna on the roof of ThutoCo and captured Moss in Carcer City.

"What do you mean?" The woman's voice sounded terrified. "We are doing our best here."

"Whatever you are doing isn't working!" Warden Ninety-Nine screamed. "He was piggybacking our comms. The breakers shut it down but that chip is running!"

MOSS GASPED FOR AIR, seeing white.

"Dad?" he croaked. His voice sounded weak and his mouth was dry. He tried to move but felt the restraints on his wrists and ankles.

He was in the program no longer.

"No, son, it's just me," Warden Ninety-Nine said, his blurry form blotting out the light as he loomed over Moss. "You cannot stop yourself from causing problems for me, can you?"

Moss thought to speak but had no words. His tongue was like leather in his mouth.

His eyes rolled around the room, adjusting to the light. Machines beeped and hissed but all he could see was unclear whiteness. From the cold sweat on his body, he knew he was naked and he felt a prick in his arm.

"What were you doing?" Ninety-Nine asked in a tone which was meant to sound conversational but struck his ear as aggressive.

Moss was weak, the temporary peace and power of the program now sapped. He wondered if it had even been real.

Even if it had, it didn't matter. Seti had said he needed to escape to be rescued, and he knew there was no hope of that.

"You know," the Warden said, moving in close. Moss was able to focus on the man. Gray was sneaking into his black mustache. His skin was burned and blotchy from sun exposure and his eyes were red and fierce. "We won't have to try to break into you if you simply speak with us."

Moss looked around the room again, the former blobs in his vision now computers and medical equipment. He saw the woman who had been speaking.

Unlike the Warden in his dark armor, she wore a white smock over scrubs and had large, kind eyes set into a dark complexion. The way she watched Ninety-Nine gave Moss the distinct impression that she didn't like the man.

He tried once more to speak, hoping to delay whatever work they planned to do on him. He tried to move his head but felt as though he was bolted to the chair.

"He needs water," the woman observed.

Ninety-Nine turned on her like a dog on an intruder. "So, get some! What, do you need a written invitation?"

Her shape receded and Moss heard a door swing open, close, and beep as it locked. He wondered how many people were on the other side of the door, watching from the cameras and behind the single reflective wall he could see from the corner of his eye.

"So hard to get good help," Ninety-Nine smirked. "Though I suppose you know that. Terrence was so easy to sway."

At the mention of Terrence, who Moss had come to know and trust as Grimy, he moved to thrash against the restraints. Grimy's betrayal of Moss and his friends to Carcer was still fresh in his mind.

The door opened again, and the woman approached and held a paper cup up to Moss's lips. He sipped at it slowly before the Warden's hand moved in and flicked the cup, splashing his face and mouth. The woman let out a little yelp as Moss gulped and sputtered.

"That was unkind," she admonished, trying to restrain her anger.

"Don't be a fool," Ninety-Nine snarled. "This kid is a terrorist. If he had it his way, this entire organization would be destroyed, and you would be dead." He turned venomous eyes on Moss. "And you call yourself *good*," he mocked.

"This man is in my care," the woman said, and Moss noticed her accent for the first time. He couldn't identify it but remembered he was in Africa and assumed it was a local way of speaking. "It would serve you well to remember that and retain some modicum of decorum."

"It would serve you well to remember that I don't report to you," he snapped.

Her eyes narrowed. "Nor I to you." She folded her arms. "You may question him, but I'll allow none of your brutish tactics here."

The Warden's face flushed an even darker red before his eyes flashed to the camera mounted in the corner of the room.

"Thank you," Moss croaked to the woman, who turned on him with surprise.

She looked guilty. "That's premature."

Moss tried to nod but remembered he was unable to move his head.

She lifted a chrome device in the shape of a gun with a vial attached at the top. "The water felt good, no doubt, but this will help with the dryness."

He felt the thing press against his arm and heard it discharge.

She put a palm against his cheek. "Now we wait a moment."

It didn't take long for saliva to return, and she turned to Ninety-Nine and nodded.

He grinned. "I'll ask you again, what were you doing?"

Moss played dumb. "When?"

The Warden took a long, self-soothing breath. "You know when and you know what I mean. She won't be able to protect you for long if you try to play me for a fool."

Moss grimaced. His time in Carcer City had made him feel as though all the Wardens were idiots who could be easily played. Warden Ninety-Nine was not. He had caught Moss and his friends twice, and Moss suspected he was the person behind the video of his grandmother that had made him want to go to C City in the first place.

"I don't know what I was doing," Moss said, the words soft and quiet in his ears.

Warden Ninety-Nine cocked an eyebrow. "Now, that I believe."

He assessed Moss a moment longer. "And you don't know how you used our comms?"

Moss willed himself not to try and shake his head. "No."

The Warden let out a long breath, bent his arms at the elbows, and stretched to crack his back.

"You know who built the system in your head?" he asked as though it was an afterthought. He had gone from aggressive to seemingly bored in an instant.

"No," Moss lied.

It seemed to work. Ninety-Nine pulled at the whiskers above his lip. "So, your family made you some kind of weapon but didn't teach you the first thing. That about right?"

Moss grimaced. There was more truth to the statement than he liked to admit. He knew he had a natural acumen for what he was doing, but when it came to his family, he was always playing catch-up.

"Yes," Moss said. He was pleased that the man seemed to believe him and be taking him at his word.

"I suppose," Ninety-Nine said with a shrug, "it'll be up to the breakers then."

The words sent a cold chill down Moss's spine. Being asked questions was one thing. He could make conscious decisions, lie, try to maintain some control. With the breakers hacking his chip, he lost any sense of power.

He knew what he wanted to do.

Closing his eyes, he willed his mind to enter the program. From there, perhaps he could take control of the security, unlock doors and use Carcer's own weapons against them.

He opened his eyes.

Warden Ninety-Nine laughed. "This isn't a bad dream."

Moss frowned.

"Put him under," Ninety-Nine ordered. "If you see any funny business, pull him out again and I'll remind him."

Though the Warden was speaking to the woman, the threat was for Moss.

The woman moved and Moss heard the rattling of devices before she approached once more.

"When you wake up," she began.

"*If* you wake up," Ninety-Nine corrected by way of intimidation.

The woman exhaled with disgust. "When you wake up, I'll be here and hopefully you won't have felt a thing," she soothed.

Ninety-Nine grunted and rolled his eyes. "If you keep coddling him," he began but was cut off.

The room was plunged into darkness.

CHAPTER 2

"Intruder alert! Intruder alert!" A robotic voice blared in the black.

Moss heard commotion and tried to look around but was entirely blind. He could make out the sound of the Warden moving toward the door, but little else.

"Get down!" Ninety-Nine's voice boomed.

Lights flickered to life and the room was bathed in a low glow.

"Backup generators online," the robotic voice informed them.

Warden Ninety-Nine did not move. His body was primed like a snake ready to strike; his weapon, gripped in a steady hand, was pointed at the door. The woman cowered in a corner of Moss's vision.

"Coastal storm," the woman offered. "Sometimes the baboons set off the alarms looking for shelter."

Ninety-Nine stood like a statue. "Possible, but I'm not taking any chances."

"My friends will come for me," Moss found himself saying.

He had told them not to and Seti had said they would not, but it made him feel good to suggest it.

"You idiots got into Carcer City because I wanted you to," Ninety-Nine said out of the corner of his mouth. "Even your grandmother, famed as she is, couldn't get in here."

His words left no doubt.

Then Moss heard something in his mind.

Zeta Six, on my mark.

He knew no one else had heard it and furrowed his brow in puzzlement. Seti had opened a line for him on a neural network that would work outside, but he knew this was coming from someplace close. The speech was militaristic and unfamiliar.

His memory flashed.

It felt like a lifetime ago that he had heard the neural commands in the burbs.

When he had first met Ynna, she had hacked his implant to allow him to hear the orders others thought. If he could hear them now, it could only mean one thing: the voices he heard were ThutoCo employees.

He tried once more to thrash but he was secured to the metal slab. Fear coursed through him. He was scared of Carcer but terrified of ThutoCo. His former employer had a vendetta against him, and he had helped to blow up one of their facilities. If they were here, they wanted him.

"Warden!" he shouted but Ninety-Nine didn't flinch.

"Not falling for it," he hissed, gun trained at the door.

Moss thought better of it. Perhaps in the coming confusion, if he was freed, he could disarm someone and make his escape.

Three, two, one, he heard in his mind's ear and the room went black once more. The woman screamed.

What followed was a confusion of activity as beam weapons flashed like a lightning storm. People moved and fell as weapons discharged. Moss watched as the Warden glowed blue for a moment when he was struck with a bolt and convulsed to the ground.

Clear, Moss heard and a flashlight broke the black, a beam pointed in his face.

Asset confirmed, another voice barked.

"Employee Moss," a woman's voice cut in as more flashlights moved to his back. "I'm Commander Ichika of BurbSec Zeta Force. I'm here to rescue you."

Moss wanted to laugh. Going from one captor to another was hardly a rescue.

Restraints off, double time, Ichika ordered. Moss felt something as one of the commandos worked at whatever device held the back of his head in place.

The blue light of a screen illuminated the mask of another, who looked to be hacking the digital locks which held his arms and legs in place.

The beam of a flashlight scanned the room and stopped, lowering before Moss heard the sound of hinges and a thud.

Personal effects acquired, a voice informed the commander. *Holy shit, he's got an off-world Dermidos in here. Pretty beat up though.*

That'll do, Ichika said. *Bag the rest.*

"Employee Moss," the Commander said and, much like Ninety-Nine, she affected a friendly, albeit hurried tone. "Once free, dress quickly. They will be swarming soon and we can get you out of here but you must do exactly as I say. Is that understood?"

"Yes," Moss rasped as he felt a jerk at the back of his head. He swayed his head side to side uneasily, happy to be free.

"Yes, ma'am," one of the others corrected Moss.

"Yes, ma'am," he said, feeling the thump of the Dermidos against his body.

He tried to count the flashlight beams as they moved, calculating his odds. He thought he saw six, but it was hard to tell. He knew he was outnumbered, however many there were. These wouldn't be slouches either. If they had broken into one of Carcer's most secure facilities, he knew it would be nearly impossible to get a leg up on them. But he had been against insurmountable odds before and pulled through, so that gave him hope.

He heard a beep and felt the restraints open.

He immediately fumbled in the dark to put on the bodysuit. His arms and legs were sore and he wondered how much surgery it had taken to heal him. He felt hands come to his aid, standing him up and zipping him into the suit. He knew that the off-world tech could make him invisible but also that Ichika knew it too.

As quickly as his body would allow, he reached for one of the gun barrels in the dark but as he gripped the metal, he felt something press against his neck.

"None of that," Ichika admonished. "We are here to rescue you, remember?"

Moss snorted.

"Now do as I say and try to keep in mind that we are your friends," she soothed, pulling the taser from his neck.

He wanted to punch her in the face. The pretense was infuriating. They both knew exactly why they were breaking him out, and he had no interest in pretending it was otherwise.

She turned back to him, the beam from her flashlight casting enough glow so that her mask was illuminated. "Ready to go?"

"Yes, ma'am," he forced, all the while trying to think of an escape. "Can I have a weapon?"

She reached up one hand and patted him on the cheek. "Not on your life."

Just knock him out, one of the commandos suggested.

Moss watched Ichika's head turn in the direction of one of the beams. *You want to carry him?*

No, ma'am, Moss heard and Ichika turned back to him.

"Follow us," she said.

Moss moved in behind her in the dark as the others fell in around him, forming a circle, guns up. Moss flinched as one put a hand on his shoulder as Ichika opened the door.

Power being rerouted, Commander, Moss heard and a moment later Ichika turned to look over her shoulder.

"That suit of yours cloaks. Activate it now if you want to live," she told Moss, and he did as instructed.

Moss watched as the vaguely illuminated figures disappeared one by one, their white armor shimmering into blackness. Flashlights went dark as they moved down a long, wide hallway.

The lights overhead turned on all at once, the sound of coursing electricity filling the space. Moss heard the shuffling of feet as they moved but saw little as he looked around, the movements mostly masked: their shapes were as looking through gas.

He noticed flashes below and noticed his pale flesh showing through bullet holes in his suit. It had been washed of blood, and he wondered why Carcer had brought it all the way here with him.

They took a hard turn at one alleyway and Moss kept expecting to see an army of Carcer guards closing in on them.

The cybermesh that covered his eyes as part of his suit automatically adjusted when the lights turned on and allowed him to see without waiting for his natural eyes to adjust. He realized he could have used night vision as soon as he was zipped in and kicked himself for possibly missing an opportunity to escape.

The hallway they navigated was wide enough for small carts to shuttle staff around. Cement walls and floors in every direction. The only adornment was propaganda posters lining the walls. They were the same as in the barracks in Carcer City, every one of them demanding dedication to the cause or asking questions of loyalty.

ThutoCo had encouraged their employees differently. Bonuses for productivity and achievements were doled out to encourage people to live their whole lives in service to the company. Moss wondered what his old mentor from the company, Mr. Greene, would have had to say about the posters.

Moss was snapped back to reality when he heard a communication in his mind. *Breakers countered. Carcer moving on your position.*

Without a weapon, Moss felt as naked as he had on the table.

Copy. One minute from the shaft, Ichika informed the voice.

Too late, coming up on your nine, the voice said, no doubt watching their progress from a computer somewhere.

Moss saw a vague shimmer as Ichika turned her head. *Be ready, weapons free*, Ichika ordered and Moss heard the slight click of firearms.

He wanted to be prepared for what was coming and planned to use the soldiers as shields to make his escape. He could run, try to find an exit but he had no idea where he was or where he was going. He felt powerless and lost.

He tried once more to will himself into the program. Perhaps Seti could give him a layout of his surroundings. The attempt only caused him to miss a step and stumble forward, catching himself on an invisible body.

"Hey!" the soldier seethed.

They stopped as they approached a hallway on their left. A hand pushed Moss to his knees.

Toss 'em, Ichika commanded and Moss covered his head as he heard the distinct sound of grenades being primed.

The sound of metal clinking and rolling echoed through the

space before people screamed out and the building shook with explosions.

Dust and debris filled the space and Ichika yelled aloud, "Go, go, go!"

Moss was nearly dragged in the opposite direction of the grenades. Bullets whirred around them and Moss watched as the Zetas fired back, their beams disappearing into the smoke.

His shoulder was pulled down as one of the commandos was hit and cried out. His armor hissed and crackled and returned to its natural flat white color.

To Moss's confusion, the man gave a thumbs-up as they moved away from him.

Then he understood.

As they moved away, leaving the man behind, smoke began to arise from his form.

A pop sound emanated from the armor, barely audible over the sound of the Carcer guards now streaming through the smoke. The armor of the felled commando began to corrode and melt from the inside, and just before they rounded another corner, nothing was left of the man but blood, chemicals, and a noxious gas.

Moss thought back to one quiet night, sitting with Stan at his favorite Chinese restaurant, eating bell peppers with beef. Stan struggled to use chopsticks with his remaining arm.

After they had set off the explosion at ThutoCo, he had taken time to teach Moss about the world. The education always included a culinary element, Stan speaking as he devoured platefuls.

"All the big companies smile in each other's faces while they stab each other in the back," he said, waving down a waitress and indicating toward the pork buns in a wooden bowl on her tray. As she set the steaming bowl before them, Stan looked at

Moss and grinned. "A man who doesn't eat pork buns can never be a whole man."

Moss smiled and rolled his eyes. "Whatever you say."

Stan reached in and pulled out a bun, ripping it in half before popping it in his mouth. Red sauce dribbled down his chin as he explained, "The corporations employ small armies, which they use against the others."

"Really?" Moss said in surprise. The only thing he had seen which even came close to approximating that was BurbSec, the local security for the burbs. His friend, the woman who gave him nothing but confusing thoughts, Issy had joined their ranks. Though she was tough, he couldn't imagine her engaging in corporate warfare.

"Yes, really," Stan said as though it were a stupid question.

Moss snorted. "But what if they get caught? How can they smile in each other's faces when there is evidence of what they are doing?"

Stan shook his head. He was always kind to Moss as he taught him the way of things, but Moss could often tell that he felt as though he was speaking to a foolish child.

"They destroy the evidence." Stan's expression was grim.

"Oh," Moss said, understanding the dark implication.

Moss never thought he would see the inter-corporation destruction of evidence about which Stan had taught him.

Defensive positions, Ichika ordered as they reached an elevator door.

Moss was forced to the ground once more as one shimmer moved to begin pulling the door open manually. No person would have the strength to part the heavy metal, and Moss realized it had to be a drudge, the robot being remotely operated by a person sitting comfortably in a hex somewhere. The door groaned against the force but did not move.

Shields up, Ichika said and Moss heard the clatter of movement before twin metal plates were placed on the ground between them and the advancing guards. The plates opened, the cloaking no longer doing its job, and they telescoped up and out, creating a thin metal wall that began glowing blue at the front.

A throng of Carcer guards rounded the corner, and the commandos around Moss began firing in quick succession. Guards dropped one after another as the beams sprayed down the hall.

The guards pulled back quickly.

I have to burn a lock, a robotic voice told them. Moss figured it was the drudge.

"Grenade!" Ichika hollered and they all ducked as three metal balls clanked down the hallway.

Moss felt his world erupt as two blasted the hallway apart.

The third exploded near the shield to his right, and a blur was blasted back, parting the dust. Moss's ears rang and he choked on the acrid smoke, his Dermidos designed for stealth rather than protection. He turned to see a red laser begin cutting a massive, industrial latch that held the elevator door closed. The machine was unfazed by the explosions.

Shouts could be heard through the ringing and bullets began to strike the shield, walls, and ceiling around them as the Carcer guards fired into the haze. The smoke glowed an eerie blue with every returning shot the commandos took.

Counter breakers trying to decloak you, a voice informed them in the chaos.

How's that door coming? Ichika demanded as she fired down the hallway.

Nearly done, the drudge told her.

Moss heard another hiss and pop and looked down to see another soldier melting into a blob on the ground by his feet, debris slowly settling on top like snow coating a puddle of gasoline.

"Stop what you are doing and return him to us, and we will let you leave unharmed!" a voice offered through the gray.

Moss instantly recognized Ninety-Nine's voice through the loudspeaker and assumed his comrades had given him a reversal drug as soon as they came upon his limp body.

He wished that ThutoCo could have at least done him the favor of killing the Warden.

Ichika answered by firing a volley of bolts down the hallway.

The drudge pulled the door open and Moss turned.

Now, it informed them.

Moss felt himself pulled toward the door as one voice offered, *I'll hold them off.*

Copy, Ichika said as Moss was dragged into the elevator shaft.

Moss had to hand it to them, they were prepared: the elevator was on the floor just below and its roof served as a floor in the shaft.

"We are in," Ichika shouted. The smoke blew in wisps as the soldiers made their way to the open door.

Blood burst through the smoke as the soldier was shot from behind, red sheen mixing with the dust. The drudge pulled its arms free and the door slammed shut. Moss panted as the machine fired up its laser once more to solder the door closed.

"You'd better fucking be worth this," Ichika seethed to Moss.

He dropped his head, overwhelmed with what his life had become. "I'm not."

Ichika and the other commando affixed rigging to the cables, and Moss wondered how much equipment they held at the back of their armor.

He looked around, seeing the soldiers ready themselves and wondered if he could make his move. They were distracted but they were still trained killers, and he was exhausted and drained. If he got one of their weapons, he could take down one but knew the drudge would react too quickly.

He was determined to make his move when they reached the top of the shaft.

He had to try something.

THE SOLDIERS CLIPPED into the rigging and Ichika pulled Moss close.

"Don't let go," she told him in a deadly serious tone and he held on to the woman for dear life. He felt the jerk as he was pulled up quickly, the internal machinery yanking them up.

Moss felt an old sensation return as he tried to keep from vomiting during the rapid ascent.

The drudge had gone first, and Moss looked up in a daze to see the laser cutting the lock.

It didn't take long before the machine finished and began to pry the doors open, the natural sunlight of early morning pouring in to fill the space with a golden hue. Moss heard a clasp unhook, a grunt and a thud outside the door as a gray figure jumped. The shadow of the soldier outside moved on the far wall of the shaft.

"Jump!" Ichika ordered.

Moss looked to her dust-covered head in shock. A thin layer of debris and charring from the explosion made her visible.

He heard her snort. "Quit suckling and jump!" she shouted, angrily this time. He resented being compared to a baby as he was being dragged against his will, but he had more important things to worry about.

The space between him and the door wasn't far, but the fall below him was.

Ichika groaned. "Here," and she lifted a foot against the cable so Moss could use her bent knee as a jumping-off point.

His eyes flashed to the weapon at her side.

"Please give me a reason to fucking kill you," she snarled.

His heart raced as he put his foot on her leg. He took a deep breath and jumped.

Forgetting his augmented legs, he miscalculated and jumped with far more force than he meant to, crashing into the commando outside.

Moss blinked up at the sun as the soldier beneath him gasped, "Asshole."

Ichika landed behind them, a fluttering trail of dust dancing in her wake.

The building shook and Moss saw the drudge look down.

They're through, the robotic voice informed them, but just as the message transmitted, the machine was ripped apart by machinegun fire.

The elevator door slammed shut and the three of them were left in an oppressive silence.

Moss was pushed to his feet as the commando under him got up. Moss turned to survey his surroundings. They appeared to be on a service parapet on the side of the massive building. It stretched up much higher and they were on what amounted to little more than a lip that terminated at the nearby corner of the building.

Moss was outside.

This is Moss! I'm outside the Carcer building. Is anyone here? he asked on the neural network, hoping that speaking to Seti wasn't a dream.

"I'm heeeere!" a voice cried as one of the strangest-looking men Moss had ever seen came swinging around the corner on a rope, firing a cone-shaped weapon at the commando. The soldier's body was blasted back with such force that he dented the elevator door.

Before the odd man even had a chance to land, Ichika loosed

her weapon and shot him. The bolt did its job, and he dropped from the rope, landing with a hard slam on the ground before them.

"Amateurs," Ichika snorted.

She pulled a dronepack from the front of her armor and turned Moss around by the shoulders.

It was just the two of them now, and Moss thought he could try to make his escape. He worried that he couldn't pull it off; her reflexes had been so fast.

Moss had some informal training in hand-to-hand combat, but it was nothing compared to these people.

As the drone wrapped metallic arms around his chest, Ichika turned him back to face him.

"I don't know who you are, but you better be fucking worth —" and then her head exploded, spraying Moss with blood and gore.

He heard himself let out a little scream.

He turned to see the man holding a smoking weapon. It hissed out a plume of steam and the man walked through with a broad grin.

"Who?" Moss stammered. "Who are you?"

PART II

CHAPTER 3

"I am Steampuck, though my friends may call me Puck. Rogue, charlatan, miscreant, and all-around ne'er-do-well. Bastard, prick, and thorn in the side of all megas. Swashbuckler, venturer, and hero of the commoner," the man said with a sweeping bow.

He had piercing blue eyes set into a tanned face with a brown mustache that framed his mouth down to his chin. He wore a crimson velvet top hat with goggles set into a leather strap at the base and a long peacock feather protruding off the left side. He had a black-and-red striped vest with shining brass buttons on under a long brown coat.

Brown suspenders were clasped with gold gears to black pants tucked into tall leather boots with five straps along the side.

"What?" Moss asked. "How?"

"What's modern is not always what is best," Puck explained in what sounded to Moss like Gibbs putting on a false English accent. "It would take a real bullet to put old Puck down."

He patted his gun, the metal cone extending from a polished wooden stock with another golden gear set into the side.

Moss was fascinated by this strange man with peculiar attire who had saved him.

Moss was now free and he would be indebted to this man for the rest of his life.

"Can you fly that thing?" Puck asked, tapping the dronepack.

Moss nodded.

"Huzzah. Follow me and we shall go someplace safe to get acquainted," the man clapped Moss on the back. He turned and strange-looking propellers with the appearance of metal and paper wings unfurled from his back. They began to whir as handlebars extended over his shoulders.

His arms spread wide in an exaggerated gesture before he gripped the bars and winked at Moss. "Willkommen! Bienvenue! Welcome to Cape City," he bellowed, and Moss turned to look over the city for the first time.

As he lifted off the ground, following Puck and his odd helicopter contraption, Moss looked over the vast city, low glass buildings and tall skyscrapers glinting gold in the morning sun. Hovels stacked on top of one stretched in every direction. Throughout the city, imposing black towers belching dark fumes loomed over all surrounding structures. There were some small parks and ponds and even from that height, Moss could see that they were filled with people. Massive barges pulled into and out of long docks stretching out from the curved shore. Flighted cars moved in computer-choreographed patterns.

As they banked and lowered, Moss saw masses of people move down congested streets. Plumes of smoke wafted from open cook fires as people carried bundles of charcoal sticks between cars, bouncing down crudely paved roads. Houses and low structures were painted vibrant colors, giving the city a distinctly different look from the monochrome of BA City in the day.

The nausea he had felt in the elevator shaft was gone as they descended, moving quickly toward what Moss knew had to be their target: an old white brick building with a semicircular balcony at the front held high will marble pillars.

A sign at the front read, "Mr. Navarro's Curios and Curiosities," painted in a fine hand.

They set down on the roof next to a wooden table with two hand-carved wooden chairs under an umbrella that flapped wildly at their approach.

"My humble home," Puck ingratiated as he tipped his hat to Moss.

Feeling as though he could breathe for the first time, Moss said, "Thank you."

The man cocked an eyebrow. "No need for all that just yet. You have raised the ire of two of the deadliest megas in the world and we will need to see you safe before we begin with the gratitude."

"Even still," Moss said, but the man simply smiled.

"Come along now," Puck said, pointing to a hatch in the roof. "Let's get you a room and a bed. My sister will see to your needs and when you are prepared, you may join me in the sitting room."

"Sounds good," Moss said, following him as he swung the hatch open. "I mostly need water."

"Then water you shall receive. Come along now."

They climbed down a ladder and passed through a door into a narrow hallway, lit with small gas lamps. Wood-paneled walls were adorned with paintings of men in suits and women in broad dresses at picnics.

Even being hunted, Moss felt a strange sense of safety in the place.

"Having no guests at the moment, I will set you up in our most luxurious of accommodations," Puck told him as he pulled a large key ring from his belt and opened a door with a flourish. "In you get," he said. "Irene will be up presently."

"Thank you," Moss said again.

Puck simply nodded and closed the door behind him.

Moss sat on the four-post bed, the down comforter billowing under his weight.

It was an odd sensation to be there. He had been hopeless just moments before. He had been rescued, saved by a stranger. Having done so little to free himself, he felt weak. Reaching out to Seti was the only thing of value he had done.

He had learned his program was much more powerful than he had realized before. He knew he needed to reunite with his grandmother and try to understand the full potential of what his family had put in his mind.

Seti? He reached out but got no answer. He looked around the room and was not surprised to find no communication array. A desk, nightstand, wardrobe with a single rose in a domed case and more beautiful paintings were all that the room contained.

He unzipped his Dermidos and pulled the mask free of his face, the smell of honeysuckle perfume mingling with that of drying blood. Sitting for so long had drained him of his remaining energy, and it was a struggle to stand and close the heavy green velvet drapes to cover the window.

A single lamp bathed the room in a yellow glow as he opened the wardrobe to find many odd and fanciful outfits. Rummaging, he discovered linen pajamas too large for his slight frame. Leaving the bodysuit in a pile on the floor, he pulled the drawstring on the pajamas as tight as he could and crawled into the bed.

It felt foolish to sleep while knowing he was being pursued, but fighting exhaustion was a losing battle and he was asleep in an instant.

. . .

HE HAD no idea how long he had slept—except that it didn't feel like long enough—when he heard a slight knock at the door.

"Mister Moss," a delicate voice asked.

Moss groaned.

"Mister Moss, may I enter? It's Irene, my brother mentioned me," she announced as though there was any doubt.

"Give me a second," he forced from his mouth. Feeling the erection, he knew he needed a moment.

"Yes, sir," Irene's voice was patient and accommodating. "I have the water you requested."

Hearing those words reminded him how parched he was, so he dragged himself from the bed, pushing down to hide his penis before realizing that the slight fabric was going to offer nothing.

"Just one more moment," he stammered before deciding he didn't really care. He needed the water desperately, and some stranger seeing him this way, while embarrassing, was the least of his concerns.

His friends were off in a fight somewhere. He was being chased and needed to come up with a plan before being taken once again. If he was caught, Moss knew that he would not be so lucky a second time.

He opened the door and before him stood a young woman in attire as fanciful as her brother's: a ruffled brown skirt draped long at the back was held up with straps at the front to expose long legs in tall boots. A crimson corset was cinched tight and accented with more golden gears. Black lace gloves stretched up to her elbows from where she held a tray with a jug of ice water with lemons.

The shoulderless white top with no sleeves or bra beneath did nothing to hide her breasts and did nothing to assuage the protuberance in his pants.

Her crystal blue eyes seemed to take no notice, though, and

he studied her face. Her slightly upturned nose and thin lips were etched with scars that covered her face. They were slight, but many and were a surprise to see.

Most people had all their scars removed unless they chose to keep them as a badge of honor or toughness. Moss thought it odd to keep them on such a pretty face and thought he might ask about it if the situation arose.

"Might I enter?" she asked quietly.

Moss flushed with embarrassment. "Of course," he said, stepping aside and turning his body away from her.

She entered and set the tray down before turning to Moss with a hand extended. She noticed then and let out a little, "Oh," before regaining composure.

"Sorry," Moss blurted awkwardly. "It's just, I just woke up, and I mean, well."

"It's no bother," she said with a giggle, trying to save the moment but only deepening his shame.

He turned fully away from her.

"Is there anything else you'll be needing?" she asked kindly.

Moss looked over his shoulder at her. "Not at the moment."

"You can turn back, silly. You have nothing to be ashamed of," she offered, her words sweet as honey.

Moss felt a rush he hadn't experienced in a long time but could not bring himself to face her. He regretted even opening the door.

"I'll join you and your brother in a bit," Moss offered, ready to be alone.

Irene let out the slightest snort. "I understand."

Moss wanted to continue to apologize but let her leave the room. She was different than the women he had known: Sandra, Ynna, and even Issy were tough. Any one of them could drop Moss with a single punch.

As she closed the door behind her quietly, he tried to parse exactly what it was. Irene was dainty, delicate, and feminine in some archaic sense. Having seen her brother in action, he presumed that she could take him down as easily as the other women in his life, but she carried herself in a way wholly unfamiliar to him.

He gulped down nearly the entire jug of water, the coldness of it burning his brain.

Hydrated but no less exhausted, he moved to the wardrobe and found some clothes which fit him, his physical excitement subsiding. He found a white button-up shirt and gray vest. A pair of checkered trousers slid onto his frame appropriately though the legs hung too far at the bottom, bunching under the balls of his feet.

He shrugged, figuring he could buy something more appropriate when the time came.

HE DIDN'T REALLY KNOW where he was going but followed the narrow hallway down a curved staircase and into a large room where Puck and Irene were sitting, steaming tea in their hands.

The room looked to Moss like a museum. A large, intricately woven ornate rug lay in the center of the room with large wooden chairs topped with crushed velvet pillows surrounding it. Stuffed animal heads looked down on them vacantly. Antique weapons lined the walls, Moss's eyes resting a moment on a large mace he had only ever seen in video games. A set of medieval armor stood watch in all four corners of the room, detailed etching coating each one.

Moss's mouth fell open as he stood amazed.

"Mister Moss," Irene said, standing.

Puck followed suit. "Don't you look dashing."

Moss looked down at himself. "Doesn't really fit," he observed.

"I rather like the cut of your jib, though the pants could do with some tailoring," Irene said. Moss shifted uncomfortably. His instincts had carried him through countless firefights, but he was stymied by the kind words of an attractive woman.

"Spot of tea?" Puck offered, pointing a flat hand to a white pot with powder blue images embossed on the side.

"Maybe something harder if you've got it?" Moss asked.

"Five o'clock somewhere as they say, eh?" Puck bellowed and laughed heartily at his own comment. Irene frowned subtly. Moss found the man's gregarious style showy and irritating, but Puck had saved his life, and he would tolerate any annoyance.

"We have some brandy," Irene offered. "Will that do?"

Moss nodded. "Sure."

"Splendid," Puck intoned, clapping his hands and raising a headache in Moss.

"You ever been to BA City?" Moss asked him.

Puck shook his head. "Can't say as I have."

"There is someone there I think you would get along with," Moss told him.

Puck winked. "You are, of course, referring to Sir James: a legend in his own right. Though perhaps not so famous, or more aptly, infamous as yourself."

Moss was surprised by the comment. He didn't think of himself as all that important in the scheme of things but nodded slightly, having to admit to himself that he *had* done some things of note. "I guess I'm known now."

He shuffled his feet and jammed his hands in his pockets.

Puck guffawed. "More than that, my boy. You have a reputation to rival my own. When Seti said you needed assistance, I was beside myself with joy at meeting a legend."

"Legend is a strong word," Moss heard himself saying. "Though we have done some stuff."

Irene approached with a glass of brown liquid. "So modest,"

she said as he pulled a hand free and took the glass, taking an inelegant drink.

"Modest indeed," Puck affirmed. "And while I believe you were referencing the incident at ThutoCo, my interest lays with Ryp The Jackr."

"Oh," Moss said. He had not expected that.

"Please sit," Irene suggested, beckoning him over to a chair. He did so.

Puck and Irene waited until Moss was seated before taking their own. "Please," Puck said. "Regale us with your tale."

"Wasn't really much to it," Moss said, now actually acting modestly.

He thought back to the time—the terror in their neighborhood as the self-described serial killer turned his attention from destroying relief aids to hacking human prostitutes with neural implants and decimating their minds.

Carcer had banked on the local fear, offering protection and making a show of launching an investigation. When it became clear that the profits they earned from the panic kept them from actually wanting to find the villain, Moss and his friends had begun a hunt of their own.

Puck and Irene listened with rapt attention as he explained their investigation.

"Fascinating," Puck exclaimed when Moss reached the conclusion. "Much like myself, you are a boon to your community."

Moss knew that was a perfect way to segue. "So, tell me about yourselves."

"Ah," Puck gasped. "As aforementioned, I am Steampuck, though you may, of course, call me Puck."

Moss, having finished the glass of brandy, held up a hand to stop him. "I got the titles. Tell me what you do here."

"You wound me, sir," Puck said, holding his hands to his chest. "The preamble is but a part of the explanation."

Moss chuckled and turned to Irene. "Maybe you can fill me in?"

She gave Moss a coy smile. "Certainly," taking a sip of her tea. "We work with our mutual acquaintance, Seti. She feeds us information and we do what we can to fight those who would seek to oppress us."

"Sic semper tyrannis!" Puck bellowed, though Irene and Moss paid him no mind.

"Anyway," she continued, sounding impatient. "We work on a smaller scale than you, doing jobs more akin to your Jackr than the one you ran at ThutoCo. More local heroes, if you will."

Moss looked at them incredulously. "I can't imagine it would take a genius to find you guys out."

Puck tapped a cane by his chair to get their attention. "Ah, yes, as to our attire: we fancy ourselves vestiges of a simpler time. As the world worships the All Mighty Screen, we are content to live as did the fathers of invention," he waxed with pride.

His gratitude to the man aside, Moss wasn't buying it. "That can't possibly be true," he asserted. "You must have distribution mesh in your clothes, or you would have been knocked unconscious by that shot you took. Also, I'm pretty sure you have a graymaker in the ceiling to dampen communications. Lastly, you yourself talk to Seti, and I know that isn't by Morse code."

Irene smiled. "As clever as advertised."

"Truly," Puck agreed. "Our desire for a simpler life does not mean we turn our backs entirely on what is available to us."

"To answer your initial question: money," Irene said.

"What?" Moss asked.

"Money," Irene repeated. "We simply pay to keep ourselves from being arrested."

"We also try not to anger Carcer in particular," Puck put in. "Until today that is."

"Oh," Moss said, guilt and fear rising in him. "If Carcer knows about you and you pissed them off today, won't they be gunning for you?"

Moss felt his heart begin to race, and his eyes darted to the door as though they were going to break in any moment.

Puck smiled. "They will, no doubt, attempt to come here."

Moss stood and shouted, "We need to get out of here!"

"Hardly," Irene said, standing to put a soothing hand on Moss's shoulder. "Things here are a little different than what you are accustomed to."

"What the fuck does that mean?" Moss asked, his fear causing him to lash out.

"That means," Irene said, pulling the glass from Moss's trembling and hand returning to the snifter to fill it. "That Carcer does not control this city the way it does yours."

Moss did not speak. He just looked at the two of them for a long moment. She brought him the glass and he had another sip. "But they have a base on the hill there."

Irene gestured for him to sit again and he did.

"You are correct," she said, returning to her seat. "They do have a base of operations here, but the city itself is run by gangs. They are funded by Bovidae Biotechnics, who employ nearly everyone here in one way or another and have little patience for Carcer intrusions. It would take an invasion army for Carcer to take this city."

Moss was reminded once again how little he knew of the world. Each time he thought he understood one aspect, another would present itself. "I suppose I assumed Carcer had some kind of global dominance for security," he admitted.

"For many cities in the west, that is quite correct," Puck

agreed. "But not for all, and certainly not for much of the rest of the planet."

"Even still, won't they send some small crew after us, like what ThutoCo did?" Moss asked. He couldn't understand why they were so calm. Both of them seemed perfectly at ease, sipping tea and ignoring the fact that two of the world's largest companies were gunning for them.

"They might," Puck said.

"But they won't get far," Irene added, her bright eyes growing dark.

Moss shook his head in disbelief. "So, we are safe-ish for now?"

"For now," Puck concurred. He leaned in toward Moss, hands resting atop the cane. "The question now becomes, what's next?"

CHAPTER 4

Moss thought about it.

"I need to talk to Seti, get out of here, see my friends, and speak with my grandmother," he blurted without thinking.

"Ah, yes," Puck said. "Sandra, another woman of renown."

"Sure," Moss said, wanting to go back to talking about how he could get home.

"Though if I'm being perfectly honest, the person I would most loved to have met was Mister Burn," Puck said, a wistful expression crossing his face.

Moss couldn't help but snort a laugh. "He would have hated you."

Irene let forth a hearty laugh before covering her mouth.

Moss regretted the unkindness. "Sorry, it's been a trying time."

"Understood," Puck said, sounding wounded. "You mentioned a desire to speak with Seti."

"Yes," Moss said, pleased that at least for the moment, Puck was listening rather than simply waiting to speak.

Puck nodded simply. "We have a communication laboratory you can utilize."

"Thank you," Moss said, standing and placing his glass on an ivory coaster.

"Oh," Puck said. "You mean to use it presently?"

"No time like the present," Moss shrugged. "Plus, despite all your assurances, I know Carcer *and* ThutoCo well enough to know they will be coming for me."

"ThutoCo has even less a foothold here than Carcer," Irene explained.

Moss shook his head, the sweat on his brow from drinking cascaded to the floor. "That may be true, but I know them and I know my value to them. If they have so much as an office in this city, they will try something."

Irene and Puck stole a glance.

"What?" Moss asked.

"ThutoCo has been all but driven out of Southern Africa," Irene explained.

"Oh?" Moss asked. "So, why the look?"

Irene looked embarrassed. Puck cleared his throat and spoke. "It just seemed a surprise that this was novel information to you."

Moss grimaced. "There are a lot of things ThutoCo left out during my education."

"Of that, I have no doubt," Puck smiled as he signaled for Moss to follow him. He led Moss down a staircase next to the one which led up to his room. "You see," he spoke as they walked down the stairs into a circular room of bookshelves cordoned off with velvet ropes attached to golden stanchions. "Michael Smith is the president of Boviedae Biotechnics who, as aforementioned, run this city, and he is the uncle of Arthur Smith."

"That's a name I know," Moss observed as he looked at four

marble busts of famed authors in the center of the room under a massive chandelier.

Puck strode over to one of the busts. "Quite right. Arthur Smith is the head of your former employer; a job for which he applied at great personal peril and by taking, sacrificed his connection to the family business here."

Moss let out a long breath. "You're saying that by taking the job at ThutoCo, he forfeited working for Boviedae Biotechnics and a position here, and now the companies don't want to work together?"

A smug look crossed Puck's face. "That *is* what I said."

"Sure," Moss said, trying to keep from rolling his eyes.

Puck flipped open one of the busts and pressed a button hidden within.

Moss laughed. "Of course."

Puck shot him a look of bemused puzzlement as one of the bookcases swung open. "Pardon?"

"Nothing," Moss said as he followed Puck into a small room of computers, wires, and screens. It was nothing like the rest of the house. There were no adornments or art, just computer equipment. The siblings' apparent disdain for technology seemed to carry over into how they treated the room itself.

Puck held out a hand toward the chair in the center of the small space. "I presume you wish to be left alone?"

"If you don't mind," Moss said, flopping into the seat.

Puck smiled graciously. "Not a bother. Simply rejoin us upstairs when your conversation is concluded."

With another sweeping gesture, he left and padded upstairs quickly.

Moss turned on the computer, and the screens bathed the room in a familiar digital glow. Moss thought it strange that the most sterile, simple room was the place in the house where he felt most at home. Seti was one of the preprogrammed contacts and he selected it, waiting as the computer ran encryption coding for a while.

Before too long, she appeared. "Moss!" she said delightedly.

"Seti!" Moss blurted. "What the hell is going on at home?"

She shook her head, her blonde hair shifting unnaturally through digital distortion. "Still trying to suss that. I know Sandra and Anders ran into some kind of problem, and Ynna and Gibbs went to help out. I keep trying to get a hold of Patch, but his mom keeps stonewalling me."

"No surprise there," Moss admitted. Jo hadn't wanted to let the crew's breaker Patchwork join them from the beginning and, after seeing what the kid had gone through in Carcer City, Moss knew it would take more than a few calls to get him back.

"I'm sorry, Moss. I keep trying to get a hold of them, but they must be in it now." Seti sounded genuinely apologetic.

"It's alright," Moss said, trying not to let his disappointment show. "I need to get home."

"I know," Seti acknowledged. "As I mentioned, we don't have too many people out there, and it's not as if you can just board a plane and go back."

Moss slumped in the chair. "Right," he exhaled.

"I'm sure Steampuck could connect you with a smuggler though," she offered.

At the mention of the name, Moss leaned back to ensure that he was gone. "Speaking of, Seti, I have to ask," he began.

She chuckled. "You can trust them. We've worked together a long time, and they are our best agents in that part of the world."

Moss nodded. "I just had to ask."

"I know," Seti said sadly. "Grimy was a tough pill for us *all* to swallow."

"Yeah," Moss said, the memory still fresh.

"He was one of the oldest members." Heartbreak coated her words. "Ynna took it pretty hard."

"I'm sure she did," Moss said. He knew that Grimy had pulled her from the gutter when she was at her lowest and that she had an affinity for him as a result.

Moss looked into the screen, wishing he could read Seti's face as he asked, "How's Judy?"

Seti's lips pulled down into a deep frown under her metal eyes. "Gone. Gone as deep underground as I've ever seen. Hide nor hair."

"I'll want to find them when I get back," Moss said.

Seti nodded. "Let me know if there is anything I can do," she offered, sounding pained at not being able to do more.

Moss thought about it; he wanted to know more, wanted to press her for information he knew she didn't have. He was stuck in a strange place with strangers, being hunted for information he didn't understand how to unlock. Even free, he felt caged.

He wanted to strike back, wanted to punish Carcer, ThutoCo, and their allies for what they did to his friends, himself, and the world. He felt useless, pointless anger rising in him.

"I'll contact you if we need anything," he said finally.

"Moss," Seti said in an uncharacteristically soft tone. "I know things are bad, but we will turn it around. Trust in me and trust in the people around you and we will be fine."

Moss hardly heard her. "Alright."

The screen went black.

Moss sat a moment, feeling lost.

He had faced harder odds: they had broken into ThutoCo, they had infiltrated a prison city. He could get out of here, but it felt insurmountable.

He sighed, took a deep breath, and closed his eyes.

"Dad," he said aloud, reaching out with his mind.

He felt something.

For a moment, he thought he saw his hex.

But as he pulled at it, scrabbling to reach it, it disappeared.

. . .

PUCK AND IRENE were sitting and enjoying steaming scones as he entered the room and, upon seeing him, stood to greet him.

"You don't have to do that," Moss told them.

Irene cocked her head. "Pardon?"

Moss smiled. "The whole standing when I walk into a room thing, you don't have to do it."

"You are a guest in our home," she stated plainly. "To do otherwise would be terribly uncouth."

Puck nodded vigorously. "Indeed. Fine manners bespeak a fine civilization."

Moss shook his head. "Fine, whatever. I mean, I won't fight you on it; it's just a little weird."

"You are the product of a world devoid of empathy," Puck said, striding toward Moss. "Your screens are walls and cameras, flags of false nations. Refinement may be lost, but it lies not six feet under as long as there are some who remember and act accordingly."

Moss thought of The Conservation and their goal of returning the world to its natural state, and the girl, little Amy, who, in some way which Moss did not quite understand, represented a future more hopeful than the present Moss knew.

Looking at Puck and Irene, he realized it was not all that different. They all wanted to lift the yoke of digital and physical oppression from the world. He did too and in that way, they were united.

Moss smiled. "It's a good philosophy."

"Noble, even," Puck suggested, pulling the end of his mustache.

At that, Moss chuckled. "Noble, even."

Puck beamed. "And what did our friend have to say?"

The question brought Moss right back to the here and now. "She said I would need a smuggler to get me home."

"Ah-ha," Puck said before taking a comically large bite of scone. After the discussion they had just had, Moss found the action peculiar, but there was little about the man that made sense to him.

Moss and Irene both shifted impatiently as they waited for him to chew, swallow, and take a slow sip of his tea. "We know a smuggler."

Moss turned to Irene incredulously. "You couldn't have just said that?"

She gave a delicate smile, which Moss found almost unbearably cute. "Wanted to let him have his moment."

"It's decided then," Puck said with finality. "Irene will take you to meet our smuggler, and I shall see what the streets are saying."

"Sure," Moss agreed. "We can't forget about Carcer."

Puck nodded. "Quite right."

"You think it is safe for me in the streets?" Moss asked, nervous about the prospect of traipsing around the city with a woman whose attire would draw more than a little attention.

"'Tis harder to strike a moving target than a stationary one, my boy," Puck said in a way which suggested he found himself to be very clever.

"Shall we away?" Irene asked.

Moss stared at her a moment. "I need a weapon and, you know," he looked to his feet, "shoes."

Puck put down his food and drink, wiping his hand on a monogrammed napkin pulled from his breast pocket. He reached into his large jacket and produced a revolver, which he looked at lovingly before handing it to Moss.

"You'll take good care of her, won't you?" he asked.

"I don't plan on using her," Moss said, jamming the gun into his waist at his back and tucking the vest over.

Puck winced. "Victoria has been in our family since time out of mind."

"I would ask if you have something that isn't an heirloom or antique, but I think I know the answer," Moss joked.

"You do," Irene affirmed as Puck left the room.

He returned quickly with a pair of shiny leather loafers.

Moss smirked. "You going to tell me the lineage of these shoes? Their parents were the finest in all the land?"

The comment elicited a laugh from Irene.

Puck looked unamused. "You jest but—" he began as Irene placed a hand on Moss's shoulder.

"Let's go before he regales you with the history of his cane," Irene said and Moss laughed as he was nearly pushed from the door, down a hallway, and out a side entrance.

The heat hit him like a shot to the face as they walked into the midday sun. Sweat beaded all over his body in an instant. He had never experienced anything like it. It was always cool in the burbs, and even when the heavy fog lifted in BA City, it was never hot.

He began to pant as Irene unfurled a purple fan.

"How?" Moss gasped.

Irene turned back to look at him with a coy smile. "I've lived here most of my life. I'm used to it."

Moss ran his hand down his wet face. "I'm not sure I could ever get used to this, and you're in a heavy skirt!"

She raised an eyebrow. "You think I should take it off?"

He hadn't meant the comment to be suggestive at all. Her reply and devilish grin made his heart race. If he hadn't been sweating already, he would have started now.

"Oh, no," he strutted. "I just meant it's hot. You're hot. Oh, no! You must be hot in that!"

She held up a hand to stop him as she smiled at his discomfiture.

"My apologies, I was simply trying to get a rise out of you," she said and she did. "For the greatest hero of our cause, you certainly get flustered easily."

Moss felt himself shrink inward at her words. "I'm hardly a hero."

"There may be rather a wide chasm between how you see yourself and how the world sees you."

He had to give her that. "Truer words," was all he could muster.

"Are you peckish at all?" she asked. "There is a western restaurant nearby where we could stop a moment and you could fill up and cool off before we proceed."

He couldn't remember the last time he ate, and getting out of the heat sounded wonderful, though he knew he would have to get used to it eventually.

"Actually," he began, thinking about Stan. His old friend had loved food and loved to teach Moss about it whenever he could. He would take Moss to restaurants around the city and tell him of his days playing with the Miners FC, traveling the world and experiencing local cuisine. "I think I would like to try whatever is popular here."

"All the easier," Irene said and turned to guide Moss up the street.

The place was alive with activity and color. The men wore light shirts and shorts and the women, light, vibrant wraps. Armed drudges with massive cattle horns affixed to their robotic heads roamed the streets. Their presence made Moss nervous, but they seemed to take no note of them.

Seeing the citizens, Moss noticed something which piqued his interest. "There is more diversity here than I expected. It looks more like BA City than the Africa I was shown in pictures."

"Oh, oh my." Irene's eyes went wide, shifting to look around nervously.

Moss felt a familiar twinge of naïveté as she continued. "That is not really a matter to be discussed. Suffice it to say, the plague, or pandemic as you call it in the west, did not affect all people equally. The disenfranchised continued to be so, and the result is what you see now. Do you take my meaning?"

Moss extrapolated what he thought she meant but wasn't sure.

She continued to speak when she saw his confusion. "The thing about disease is that it doesn't care if you are rich or poor or anything about you, it simply infects. But this does not mean that everyone gets a fair shake.

"The poor were not given the same access to safety or medical treatment, and even as the plague came to an end, they were not provided supplies and aid. Many died as a result of—if not because of—the disease."

"I see," Moss said, beginning to see the tragedy of it. He had already wanted to find out more about the pandemic and ThutoCo's role in causing it, and hearing this only made that desire stronger.

They pushed through a crowd of people gathered around an entertainment pillar with holoprojections of various programs. News, stories, and competitions flashed, every one with the D2E logo in the corner.

Moss gasped for air in the heat, for the first time taking note of the odor which seemed to coat the city.

"What's that smell?" Moss asked as they neared a two-story building at the corner, the top level painted with images of faces coated in tribal tattoos.

"Follow me inside and we can speak of the aroma," Irene

said as they crossed the street and passed through double doors under the words "We Are Africa Restaurant."

They were greeted by a tired-looking maître d' with false tattoos painted on his face.

"Good day, Irene," he said lazily, looking up only briefly from his palmscreen before returning to watch yellow-and-black-uniformed players kick the ball upfield.

"Greetings, Mo, how are you this very fine day?" she asked, undeterred by his disinterest.

"Shit job means my children eat this *very fine day*," he snorted in the same accent which Moss recognized from the woman helping Warden Ninety-Nine.

Irene blanched as he threw her words back at her but regained her composure quickly. "Table for two, please."

The restaurant was full of people at tables enjoying meals and taking pictures of the stucco walls covered in local art. Moss presumed the place to be a tourist hangout.

The man waved a hand absently toward an open table, and Irene clicked her tongue disapprovingly before guiding Moss into the restaurant. They sat at chairs of which the arms were carved into the shapes of various animals that Moss did not recognize but wanted to know more about.

A young woman with a shaved head approached and handed them menus with a broad smile.

Irene waved the menus away. "No need," she said. "We shall take the sampler platter. My friend here is from out of town."

The girl laughed. "Everyone in here is from out of town," she noted, folding the menus under her arm and affirming Moss's suspicion. As she scampered away, Irene looked to Moss.

"Pleased to be out of the heat?" she asked with a kind smile.

"Very," Moss said, almost cold now as the air conditioning cooled his sweat. "So, about the stench?"

"Right," she nodded. "Admittedly, I hardly notice it anymore."

"Hard to imagine, the whole place smells like shit," Moss put bluntly.

The corner of Irene's mouth turned up slightly. "Though vulgar, you are actually quite right. What you are smelling is cattle excrement from the koeitoring."

Moss gave her a blank look.

"You saw the large towers all about the city?" she asked and he nodded. "Those are bioengineering facilities where they create and raise the cattle. Waste is composted and creates fertilizer. It is a profitable endeavor, but. . ." she trailed off.

"Ah," Moss said, understanding. "I'm surprised I didn't see more hamburger places on the walk over here."

Irene looked at him the way Stan used to. "The products the citizens produce are not sold to the citizens."

"Of course," Moss said, feeling foolish.

"The beef is sold to the off-world colonies, as is the fertilizer. The people here live in excruciating poverty so somewhere in the stars a person can pay exorbitant prices for *their* hamburger."

"Same old story," Moss said.

Irene frowned. "Quite. Why we do what we do," she said.

Silence descended on the two.

"Moss," Irene said, looking into his eyes. Even the simple use of his name caused his breath to shorten.

"Yes?" he said.

Her face contorted slightly as she seemed to grasp for the right words. "Might I, may I ask you about yourself? Your name is on the lips of all those who seek to free this world, but the man who sits before me seems so very different from him of whom I've heard."

Moss smiled slightly. "I'm sure, and yeah, ask away."

"How did you come to live this life?" she asked, seeming shy and nervous about asking.

Moss shrugged, not knowing how to answer the question. "It's been a weird road," he admitted. When she said nothing, he continued, "I was what in the west is called a "bub," meaning I was raised in a burb, a corporate housing structure for ThutoCo employees.

"I had a normal childhood of school and friends but had no idea that my parents were working as inside agents trying to take down the company while my grandmother on my father's side was building a team to help them.

"As happens, the company found out and took my parents in the night. They tortured and killed them and wiped my memory of the whole thing."

Irene, who had been covering her mouth, looked at him with misty eyes. "Tragic," she said. "Why did they not kill you too, I wonder?"

A shot ran through him at the question. "Irene, I've asked myself that very question every day since I found out," he admitted. He had never understood why he had been lucky enough to have survived. "I think they wanted to think they were above killing children. At the time, anyway."

"Oh, my," Irene said.

Moss realized he felt the same about her as she did about him. She had said he didn't match his reputation, and he was having a difficult time believing that a woman with such delicate sensibilities was also a hardened agent for their revolution.

"So," she said, clearing her throat softly. "You were sent to an orphanage?"

Moss couldn't help but laugh, feeling for the first time that he understood things better than someone. "Oh, no. The company raised me," he explained.

She tilted her head and dropped her hands, one gloved

finger brushing up against Moss's, causing his heart to flutter. "How does a company raise a child?"

"Pretty common, really," Moss told her, all the while thinking about their hands. "They give you a room and a place in the school, and a BurbSec Truant Officer checks to make sure you are in by curfew."

Though it felt so natural to him, Irene looked appalled. She placed one gloved hand on top of his. The touch felt nice. After so much hardship and brutalizing actions, human affection was wonderful. His heart began to race.

He was in love with Issy and he knew it, but she was far away and had still not forgiven him. It was trying, and the soft touch of a kind woman was enough to make him forget, if just for that moment.

"While a company may be able to keep a child alive," she said, her clear eyes staring into his soul. "It sounds rather devoid of love."

He dropped his head, but she reached across the table with her free hand and lifted him by the chin.

He gave her a weak smile. "It was, in some ways. But I found love in other ways. My friends became the family I had lost. I found a mentor who took me under his wing and taught me how to succeed at work and. . ." he paused, not wanting to admit.

"And?" She pressed sweetly.

"I became close with an AI that I worked with. My drudge companion became one of my closest friends. It just sounds sad now," he nearly whispered.

She put a hand on his cheek, her eyes wide and kind. "A boy who lost his family finding a connection wherever he can isn't sad. It's natural."

"Thank you for saying that," Moss croaked, overwhelmed with emotion.

He had connected to his friends since leaving the burb, and

Gibbs was always there for him when he needed someone to lean on, but speaking with Irene was different. She was interested and kind and exactly what Moss needed at that moment, though he hadn't even known it.

"And did you ever find any other kind of love?" she asked, and once again, he felt the flutter.

"Yes, sorta, I don't know," he said, his own words sounding weak in his ears.

He exhaled deeply and let the moment sit before shaking his head. "Then one day, Ynna found me and told me everything, and the rest, as they say, is history."

Irene let out a little chuckle. "What you have told me makes it all the more difficult to parse how you became some feared fighter."

Moss laughed too. "Right? Puts to bed the whole nature-versus-nurture debate."

"I suppose it does," Irene agreed. "Seti mentioned you have some program in your mind."

Moss let out a little snort. "Well, in my implant anyway. I'd like to think my mind is still my own."

"You certainly seem to be your own man," she said graciously. "This program, what does it do?"

He wanted to know the same thing. "I wish I could tell you."

"Oh," she said, obviously surprised by his answer. "You don't know, yourself?"

Moss shook his head as the waitress appeared with a sizzling plate of meat and vegetables on top of a wooden platter.

She set it down and began pointing. "Crocodile, ostrich, giraffe, lion, kudu, wildebeest, and warthog."

Moss looked up at her with a smile. "I love animals but don't even know what half those things are."

She smiled back. "A taste of Africa."

As she left, he looked at Irene questioningly.

"They are animals who used to live wild around here but which are now cloned and butchered locally for tourists so they may go home and tell their friends what they have eaten," she informed him.

Holding up a piece of strange meat on his fork, he chuckled. "When I said I wanted to eat local, I meant what the locals actually eat."

She flushed. "My apologies, I'm sure we could." He held up a hand to stop her.

"I was just teasing," he said. "I'm sure this kudu will be delicious."

"You're too kind," she said softly. "So, you don't know anything about this program?"

He shrugged as he put a piece of meat in his mouth and, to his great surprise, it was delicious. "Not really. I'm still learning," he spoke with his mouth full.

He swallowed and looked at her, her eyes not having left his. "Now, I want to know more about you. How did you come to live here and like this?"

He couldn't read the expression on her face. "Nothing much to tell, really. My brother and I lived in London until our father's business brought us here. He was killed in an accident at work, and we were left destitute when the company claimed his death was his own fault. Mother took to drink and died but a few years later.

"We vowed that no others should experience what we did and began the work we now do. Started small, but when Seti got wind, she brought us into the fold."

She began nibbling at a leek.

"And the clothes, the lifestyle, the shop—which, by the way, I still haven't seen the inside of," he noted.

"When father died, mother sequestered herself away from

us. We had no power so we would sit by candlelight and read stories of old, becoming rather obsessed with a bygone era.

"Over time, escapism became a lifestyle as we began to dress and live like the characters in our beloved stories. And the rest, as they say, is history."

She shot him a clever smile.

"Very nice," he said.

"Now eat up," she ordered, though it sounded to Moss like a question. "Your friends await, and we have a smuggler to meet."

CHAPTER 5

Moss pushed the small plate of Malva pudding away, unable to eat another bite.

"What do I need to know about this smuggler?" he asked, hoping the answer was that they were kind and generous, but knowing it wouldn't be.

"She's a kind and generous woman," Irene joked. Moss thought about Anders, the only smuggler he had ever met, realizing he actually was those things.

"I jest, of course," Irene said and took a little forkful of Moss's dessert. "She is tough but has always treated me with kindness and my brother, a little too much kindness if you take my meaning."

Moss laughed. "I do. That why it's you taking me to meet her?"

"Yes," Irene said plainly. "She is leery of new people so perhaps you could let me do the talking?"

"Of course," Moss said. "I have no plans to say anything."

"You continue to surprise me," she said.

. . .

IRENE PAID and they were back on the sweltering streets in no time. The familiar buzz of overhead drones delivering goods and packages was drowned out by street vendors hollering about their products. "Genuine giraffe pelts," "Local beer," and "Cheap augments," combined into a confused din.

Sweat dropped into Moss's eyes as they approached a warehouse where armed men and women in neo-gothic attire loaded trucks labeled "Baz's Shipping."

One woman looked up at them and called out to a man smoking in a van parked parallel to the warehouse. "Let them through."

The driver flicked the cigarette onto the ground in a spray of embers and reversed the van to reveal a door. Irene gave a courteous wave and guided Moss into the building where drudges were lifting and sorting heavy crates. A plastic table of projected screens was set at the center, and a voice called out from behind.

"Your brother too chicken shit to come himself?" the voice asked.

Irene scoffed. "Ever the charmer."

A woman stood behind the screens, her skin obsidian black. It was not a natural dark but a bioaugmented pigment. Her cybernetic eyes were also black, and she wore a black leather bodysuit covered in zippers with a knife protruding from the front like a penis. Her hair was microdyed a dark red and pulsed to look like blood cascading down to her shoulders.

It was a look that was no doubt designed to be intimidating, and it worked. Moss stopped moving as she stood.

"Guessing you're here on business since Puck takes all the pleasure," she said, striding around the table, tall heeled shoes clicking as she moved.

"Quite right," Irene said. "My brother sends his warmest regards."

The woman snorted. "There's enough bullshit in this town without you piling it on."

Moss had to smirk at that.

"Who's your friend?" she asked, turning to Moss with eyes that spun and focused, analyzing him, feeding information directly to her brain.

Irene held a hand toward him as though he were a product for sale. "This is Moss, a friend of ours who desires passage to BA."

She looked at him dubiously before extending a hand. "I'm Baz," she said, before adding, "but we are all Baz here."

"Nice to meet you," Moss said as she scraped a long red fingernail along his palm when she released his hand. A cold chill ran down his spine.

"I'm sure it *is* nice to meet me since you want something from me," Baz asserted.

Irene moved closer. "We can pay," she offered.

Baz snorted a false laugh. "Money I've got, Scarface. You know better than to come in here just offering that."

"Worth a shot," Irene said, pretending not to be bothered by Baz's comment, but Moss could see the anger in her eyes.

"A quid pro quo then?" Irene asked.

Baz smiled, revealing red teeth set into black gums. "Fuckin' a right. You think I'm going to waste an opportunity for some free labor, you don't know me at all."

"Oh, I know you," Irene said and for the first time, Moss got a flash of the toughness he knew her to possess. A simple comment rang like a veiled threat.

"You keep telling yourself that, sweetpea," Baz said, shifting her weight so the knife faced Irene.

Moss hated the tension of the exchange and said, "What is it that we can do for you?"

Irene and Baz both turned their attention to him instantly. He wondered if he had misjudged the moment.

Baz grinned again. "I like a man who gets right to the fucking point."

Moss spoke without thinking. "Then I'm surprised you like Puck."

Irene's eyes went wide but Baz let out a genuine laugh. "The man *can* fucking bloviate," she smiled, stepping toward Moss. "Your new friend's got balls, saying that shit in front of you," she said to Irene before grabbing Moss's crotch and turning to face him. "Now let's see you use them."

Moss had never been manhandled like that before, and his breath caught in his lungs.

"Please unhand him," Irene suggested with a seething undertone.

Baz smiled viciously. "Your wish," she said, and pulled away, letting the moment hang.

For the first time in a long while, Moss wished he was back in his hex, home and away from the confusion of the world in which he found himself. His simple life on rails seemed so distant now, like a dream or some false reality. But there was an appeal to it all, to the boring sameness of a life unlived.

He shook the thought from his mind as Irene asked, "What is it we can do for you?"

"Simple, really," Baz stated. "I need you to intercept a vial which is being transported this evening from a lab to Tower Twenty."

Irene laughed theatrically. "Simple, you say?"

"For someone of your skills, sure," Baz told her. "I'll print you the information since you can't just get with the fucking times."

"Grim times lead to grim lives," Irene said stoically.

Baz snorted. "Don't fucking proselytize to me. Using a quill when computers exist is as asinine as it is antiquated."

Moss smirked. He couldn't help but wonder how Baz and Puck came together. Gibbs always argued that "opposites attract," when going after girls out of his league, but these opposites seemed outright incompatible.

Baz stepped back behind the screens before an ancient printer buzzed to life, sending a cloud of dust into the air as it began to work. She stepped over and pulled the paper, handing it to Irene. "You don't have much time. Get me what I want, and your little friend will be on the next ship to Baa City," saying "baa," as the bleat of a sheep.

"We will away," Irene said, scanning the paper quickly before tucking it between her breasts. "A pleasure, as ever."

Baz waved a dismissive hand. "Yeah, yeah."

THE AIR HAD COOLED some as the sun tucked away for the night beyond the horizon.

"What are we up against?" Moss asked as they made their way back toward the house.

Irene sighed. "Rather a daunting task."

Unsurprised, Moss nodded. "What's with the vial?"

"Bull semen," Irene told him.

Moss nearly choked. "Bull semen?"

"You desire the long or short explanation?" she asked as they walked past some street performers juggling flaming chainsaws before a delighted and horrified crowd.

"We've got time," he said ironically.

"As I've stated, cattle is the trade of the town but most of what is produced is sent off-world. This means there is a large black market for beef, and people will pay a premium. Bovidae

Biotechnics tries to quell the flow so there is always a great demand for bull semen."

"That was the long version?" Moss joked.

Irene looked at him flatly. "Such as it is."

Moss smiled and repeated, "So, what will we be up against?"

"That is where the matter grows in complexity: the neighborhood gang will not tolerate theft in their area of influence so if they see us, they will try to stop us.

"Additionally, the company security is... unique," she trailed off ominously.

Moss stared at her. "As opposed to the completely routine activity of stealing cow jizz?"

She shook her head. "Cows are female."

Moss laughed at the absurdity of it all as they passed a small manmade lake, fenced off with a pay station at the door. Men and women sat along the cement shore casting fishing lines while a cloning tank thrummed before depositing a fish into the water. Moss noted that it must have been a rare type for the surrounding people whooped as the fish entered the murky water.

"What makes them unique?" he asked as the white building came into view.

"They are genetically modified, given stims and growth hormones from a young age. They are taller, broader, stronger, and angrier than the average person. Many are augmented and all have horns fused to their skulls as a show of dedication to the company," she explained, and Moss pictured what she was describing with increasing horror.

"Can't anything be easy?" Moss groused, rubbing his temples.

Irene smiled and put a hand on his shoulder as they approached the side door to the house. "Easy is hardly fun."

Moss chuckled uneasily, very aware of her touch. "Spoken

like a true heroine of the fight. But you must remember that up until a year ago, the closest I got to anything like this was video games."

She gave his shoulder a little squeeze. "And look how far you've come."

He knew she meant it as a compliment but as he saw it, he had let a friend get killed in Carcer City before being captured and escaped by luck rather than his actions.

A wobbly smile crossed his lips. "Thanks" was all he could muster.

She leaned in and gave him the slightest kiss on the cheek before producing a small handkerchief to wipe his sweat from her lips. He felt himself flush as he had when she first came upon him in his room, and he was sure she noticed.

"You'll do great," she said, opening the door and disappearing within.

He stood on the doorstep, his mind swimming.

He had only known her a few hours but felt an instant connection he could not quite explain. She was easy to talk to and, though they were different in so many ways, they seemed similar in the ones that mattered to him.

Back home, things were so confused and complicated with Issy. He had been in love with her his whole life, but things between them had changed so drastically, he didn't know what he felt.

He pushed the thoughts from his mind. He had much more immediate concerns and matters of the heart would have to wait, but despite himself, he thought of nothing but that kiss as he entered the building.

"WELL, we are up a creek now, eh, boy?" Puck said to Moss after Irene finished explaining the situation.

"Certainly seems that way," Moss admitted. "You two do anything like this before?"

Puck grinned. "Why, certainly."

"Right, how do we do it, then?" Moss asked.

"We assault the caravan en route and steal their goods," Irene said simply. "Perhaps they will have more than just the one sample."

"A boon that would be!" Puck agreed.

Moss looked at them dubiously. "I know you guys don't love tech but do you have a breaker? Maybe we could hack the system, stop the caravan, and unlock some doors. Might make things easier for us?"

Puck scoffed. "Your reliance on whatsits and widgets is folly. Explosives and bolt cutters have worked since time immemorial."

It was Moss's turn to scoff. "Why not rise to the level of the enemy?"

"Stoop to their level, more like," Puck said, and Moss realized this was a losing argument. Puck was dedicated to a lifestyle, and Moss knew the man could not be persuaded. Moss wanted to point out once more that they obviously used modern technology when they needed to and they had provided him with a dronepack but let the issue rest.

"Your Dermidos has been patched and is drying on the roof," Irene told him. That, at least, was something. "Perhaps invisibility will aid us?"

"I would think so," Moss said. "Guessing you don't have a Kingfisher lying around?"

Puck rolled his eyes and sighed in dramatic fashion. "Victoria will do more to stop the brutes against whom we are up than any newfangled laserbeam."

"Right, but my cloaking you have no problem with," Moss

snorted. He couldn't put his finger on why Puck was constantly able to get a rise out of him.

"Perhaps we could engage in a debate on the evils of technology after," Irene offered, to cut the tension.

Puck hooted. "And a lively row it will be!"

Moss shook his head and laughed. A year earlier he had been living a boring life in which his daily highlight was watching a VR reality competition show, and now he was in Africa, planning a heist of bull semen with two people who thought they lived in Victorian England. The absurdity of it all was too much, and he wondered what the old him, sitting in his little hex would think of it all.

"You get yourself kitted up and return post-haste," Puck ordered. "We have nary a moment to waste and much planning before we proceed."

"Sure," Moss said, moving to head upstairs.

He reminded himself why he was doing this: to get home.

CHAPTER 6

M oss crouched, his heart racing, waiting for the armored transport to come into view. The wait was excruciating, and he just wanted to get the action over with.

He took a deep breath to calm his nerves.

Puck had explained that Bovidae Biotechnics preferred ground vehicles since the local gangs were bought and paid for and offered much more protection on the streets than in the air. Moss could understand that as he had recently robbed a flighted transport easily. They had picked this section of road because it was flanked by warehouses and small farms and was unlikely to be patrolled by the gangs.

Despite their assurances, Moss couldn't shake the fear that Carcer and ThutoCo were out looking for him and that by pulling this job, they would be able to find him.

Lights from a vehicle moved slowly around the corner, and Moss knew the time was now. The transport looked more like a tank than a normal van: heavy plates covered the flat sides, thick bars crossed over the windshield and the tires were massive and thick. The lights shifted up and down as the van bounced over the uneven road.

71

Large black-and-white shapes filled the road, and the van skidded to a stop, sending a plume of dust into the night air. Moss was comfortable inside the thermoregulated suit, though the temperature had dropped once the sun had set.

Puck, dressed in the rags of a poor shepherd, ran after the ostriches they had rented, sending the massive birds scattering all around the van. He yelled to them in a local dialect he had bragged about knowing as the driver in the van laid on his horn, only further confusing the animals.

The merchant had warned them that they would pay for any damage to the animals though Moss was more concerned with their wellbeing than any cost.

He cloaked himself and made his way down toward the van as a guard stepped out from the passenger side door. The man, if he could so be called, lived up to Irene's description. He was a hulking brute with massive robotic legs, plastic tubes pumping a constant flow of stims into muscles that pulled his skin taut, and horns cresting from his head above eyes red with fury.

He screamed at Puck, waving his arms as he told him to clear the road.

The birds continued to twirl and clap their beaks in confusion as a woman jumped from the back door, pointing a gun at Puck, who continued to play his part, bowing, apologizing, and attempting to corral the animals.

The woman wore no top, her chest appearing to have pectoral muscles rather than breasts. Long, vascular arms glistened with sweat in the dim light, and large rings that pierced her flesh rattled against one another.

Moss crept toward the van, the confusion of dust and movement doing as much to hide him as the cloaking of his suit.

He knew there would be more guards inside the van, and he kept his weapon at the ready.

"Aim for the head," was what Puck kept reminding him as they had prepared for the mission.

One thug was moving toward Puck, and Moss knew his time was growing short.

The huge toes of the birds stomped around him as he approached, one rearing up to kick as he bumped into the powerful appendage. It knocked the wind out of him and he heard a shout. The dust made it nearly impossible to see as he groped his way, gasping and sputtering, toward the van.

The back of the van came into view and Moss pulled himself up, seeing two more of the massive people in the back. The van shifted slightly against his weight and their heads turned to look in his direction, seeing nothing.

"Now!" Puck called out as he pulled his blunderbuss from under his cloak and blasted the thug in the face. Blood exploded everywhere as one of the ostriches stood upright, a knifed arm appearing and stabbing the other guard in the back.

Irene had been so proud of her costume, making Moss watch as she paraded about in an impression of a bird. When he had pointed out that her legs bent the wrong way and it would be a dead giveaway, she had assured him that, "In the chaos, the guards will take no note of that."

She had been right and had taken the guard completely unaware. The knife sank hard into the guard's back, but she wheeled around and swung wildly with massive arms, knocking the costumed Irene back into the throng of birds.

As Moss hoisted himself into the van, the guards in the back stood to investigate the commotion, but the driver, no doubt seeing the scene unfolding before him, accelerated hard. Moss was thrown from the van, landing hard on the ground.

He heard what he took to be bird screams as the vehicle plowed into the animals before crunching to a stop. Hardly able to breathe, Moss forced himself to the ground. Puck was manually reloading his one-shot gun as Irene attempted to dodge and parry the advancing thug. The brute had dropped her gun when stabbed and was now slapping and punching at Irene.

The costume limited her movement and Irene slashed with the long knife, spraying blood with each stroke. The horned woman was undeterred and continued to advance viciously.

Moss tried to take aim but there was too much movement to get a clean shot.

"The fuck?" Moss heard a man growl, and he turned to see one of the guards looking in his direction.

"Shit," Moss gasped as he realized the guards could see his gun floating in the air.

The brute lowered his head and charged toward Moss, shouting to the other guards, "We've got a cloaker!"

Moss fired several shots at the approaching horns, and the man stuttered and fell right before his feet. Before he could take a breath, the other leaped over his fallen friend and grabbed Moss's wrist just behind the gun.

He didn't have time to curse before he was lifted by his arm high into the air. The force of the pull caused his shoulder to pop, and he let out a scream that alerted the brute to the position of his face. He felt a grip like a vice close around his face. He kicked his feet uselessly and flailed about as the pain became excruciating.

His vision blurred and he twitched his thumb to control the Dermidos.

He heard the crackle and smelled burning flesh as the suit sent a current along the exterior. The guard howled and Moss thudded to the ground once more. He reached with his good hand and pried the gun free.

He fired one shot, the bullet cracking one of the guard's horns. He grunted in anger and moved to grab Moss again. He fired one more shot into the beasts' face and watched as his eyes crossed as though looking for the wound.

Moss tried to scramble backward but with only one functioning arm, he didn't get clear in time, and the massive form fell upon him.

He heard Puck's gun discharge and another scream followed.

Pressing on the shoulders of the giant on top of him, he forced himself free and staggered to his feet to see his allies still in combat with the final guard. The birds were all gone, and Moss realized Puck had shot the driver.

Irene was perched on the back of the guard, trying to stab as the beast spun and punched. Moss hobbled through the cloud of dust as the two women grunted. He leveled the weapon with his weak arm.

"Irene!" he shouted and both women turned to look at him. Irene leaped backward, landing on the padding of her costume as Moss fired a shot, which grazed the guard's temple. A trickle of blood parted the dirt on her forehead, and her eyes went wide as she rushed toward Moss, who pulled the trigger to discover all the rounds had been fired.

Irene jumped to her feet and sprang toward the guard, sinking her knife between the shoulder blades and stopping her dead.

The woman groaned and reached around to her back with terror on her face. She looked at Moss as the reality set in and fell to her knees before slumping to the ground.

"Come, now," Irene ordered as she rushed by Moss toward the back of the van.

Moss tried to get his bearings; it had all happened so fast.

Large feathers wafted through the air in a slight breeze, and Moss was careful not to look at the front of the vehicle. He heard a faint sound of engines revving, and he hustled as quickly as he could toward Irene. She was using large bolt cutters to open a refrigeration unit in the back of the dimly lit van. The lock crunched and popped open.

"Sounds as if the gangs got wise," Puck announced as he strode over, standing at the rear of the van with balled fists on his hips.

Moss grunted with annoyance. "If you had just let me bring my dronepack," he began.

"You would have been spotted all the sooner," Puck stated.

Moss muttered under his breath, "A fucking Kingfisher could have cloaked."

"What's that, lad?" Puck asked, cupping a hand to his ear.

Irene turned and jammed a metal box covered in biosecurity stickers in Moss's arm. "Perhaps you could compare genitalia later? We must get away from here presently!"

Moss noted an unusual ire in her voice. The comment made him angry. He felt it was unfair to accuse him that way, but then he saw lights cascading along the buildings in their direction. Still unable to move one arm and holding the box with the other, he asked, "Can you reload this for me?"

Puck pulled the gun from his hand with love, stroking it a moment before reloading it. Puck grabbed the sample case from Moss before handing back Victoria. "Let's, as you say, get the fuck out of here."

Moss couldn't help but smile as the impression of him was uncanny.

They began to run through the streets as they heard the engines closing in on them.

As they ducked into an alley, Puck said over his shoulder, "You'll owe us the cost of those birds."

Moss scoffed, "You're thinking about that now?"

Moss had been there for the negotiations and knew the animals hadn't come cheap, their owner explaining that even cloned wildlife was hard to come by. The case under Puck's arm was a testimony to that fact.

Moss looked back to see two ATVs pursuing them up the street. Irene had told him that this territory was run by a gang called the "Safaris," and their look lived up to the name: all of the members hanging off the vehicles with long rifles in hand were wearing khaki shorts with off-white button-up shirts, tall socks, and brimmed hats.

They fired from the moving vehicles, and Puck shot back, the weapon booming in their direction but only striking the wall of a building. Moss fired two shots, trying to conserve ammunition, and heard someone call out in pain.

The Safaris were closing in fast and bullets whizzed around them as the pursuers kept up their volley.

"Oh, bollocks!" Puck cried out as he appeared to be shot in the leg, dropping the case and falling to his knees.

Irene looked back. "Get him up," she called to Moss, who did as he was told.

Moss fumbled a moment with all the cloth Puck was wearing before getting him to his feet. They hobbled past Irene, who stood by a support beam precariously holding up a freshly constructed bit of wall, the handles of her bolt cutter in each hand.

The lights were blinding as the vehicles roared up the street toward them.

Irene swung.

Crack.

The gangsters fired more shots.

Crack.

The Safaris were nearly upon them now.

Crack.

Irene dove toward them as the wall crashed to the street in a plume of debris, trapping the Safaris on the other side. They cried out curses as their vehicles skidded to a stop.

When Puck had explained the plan, Moss had scoffed. "All these costumes and traps are ridiculous and outdated."

Puck had only laughed, saying, "A wink's as good as a nod to a blind man."

Moss had found the answer patronizing and meaningless, but seeing how the schemes had worked, had to give the two credit. Moss and his friends back home were so dependent on tech and toys, but these old methods worked just as well.

The lights began to turn beyond the rubble, and they heard some of the gangsters begin to scrabble up the broken wall. Heads appeared briefly but dropped away as Moss shot at the first who reached the top.

Irene guided them into a condemned building that had an access point to a tunnel system for a long-abandoned rail line. As she pushed hard on the rusted door, Moss looked up the street to see if the gangsters had made it around. In dim blue light, he thought he saw a logo he recognized but couldn't be sure as he was pushed inside.

Irene forced the door shut and they all panted, feeling safe for the first time in what felt like a long time.

It was dark in the room with little more than moonlight streaking in through cracked windows, providing some visibility. It was enough so that Moss could see the excited light in Irene's eyes.

She balled her fists and vibrated enthusiastically. "We did it!"

Moss, with his floppy arm, and Puck, with his bullet wound, stared at her blankly.

"Come now," she grinned. "That was exhilarating!"

Moss couldn't help but smile. "That's one word for it."

"Alright Gloomy Gus, let's get you back and patched and we shall celebrate," she announced, her jubilance undeterred by the two men. She turned to head in the direction of the tunnels, but Moss put a hand on her arm.

She turned back, the white light of the moon glinting in her eyes.

"I will never be able to thank the two of you for what you have done for me," Moss said softly. "You've put yourselves in great danger to help a stranger and it means a lot.

"I know you both think of me as some hero or whatever, but I'm really just some guy who needed a lot of help, and you both have provided it without question. It's incredible and I will never forget it."

Puck clapped him on the shoulder. "You are too kind," he said with a smile. "But I have a bullet in my bum that I would rather like to see mended."

"Sure." Moss smiled.

Irene took a quiet breath. "Thank you for saying all that," she told Moss. "You must remember: We know what you are trying to do for this world, even if the world does not."

Fear, adrenaline, and excitement coursed through him at the words, and he wanted to grab Irene right then and there.

"I *am* bleeding, I'll remind you," Puck interjected, and the moment passed.

Semen in hand, they went back to the house.

CHAPTER 7

I rene had popped Moss's shoulder back into place and tended to her brother's wound. The painkillers had taken effect, and Puck lay on the couch, snoring quietly.

"Champagne?" Irene offered Moss.

He nodded slowly. "We *are* celebrating."

"Quite," she said before disappearing from the room and returning with two glasses and a large green bottle. She sat beside him on the couch, handing him a glass and popping the cork quietly, checking to make sure it didn't wake her brother. She filled their glasses and set the bottle on the floor, Moss watching as it sweated onto the fine mahogany.

"To freedom," she said, holding forth her glass.

Moss smiled. "I'll always drink to that," he told her. "To freedom."

They clinked their glasses quietly, both looking sidelong at Puck.

The cool bubbles washed over Moss's tongue, and despite everything, he felt relaxed.

Irene took a sip before setting down her glass and pulling her hair free of the ties which held it in place. As her hair cascaded down around her face, Moss sat in awe of how gorgeous she was. He had noticed the moment they met, but now, in the dim light of the flickering lamps, he was dumbfounded by her elegant beauty.

She caught him staring, her eyes dancing as she investigated his. "Yes?"

Moss looked away and took another sip before stammering, "Oh, it's, um, I— I don't know. Nothing."

She chuckled lightly. "You're cute."

He shook his head. He had been called many things in his life, but cute had never been one of them. "Thanks," he said, but it sounded more like a question. "You are a very attractive woman." The words were stilted and awkward.

He looked up to see her smiling. "Thank you," she said, tucking her hair behind an ear. "You'll leave as soon as you can?"

The question struck Moss hard. He had worked so hard to get back home as quickly as he could, but, sitting with her in this elegant room, he didn't want to leave.

He nodded. "Yes. We have a lot to do, and I only just recently discovered that my grandmother was still alive. After being captured, I figured I would never see her again but now I can."

"Family is important. I don't know where I would be without my brother. Or he without me, more accurately," Irene said quietly.

"I've been without a family for so long, I have so many questions and feel like I've never really known any of them," Moss admitted. "You guys could come with me. We could use more capable people back in BA."

"No," Irene said, running her finger along the rim of her glass. "Our lives are here. Just as you have your causes, we have ours."

Moss nodded, both saddened and relieved by the answer. His feelings for both Issy and the woman before him were confusing enough without the complication of them being in the same place. "Then it was a pleasure meeting you," he said, extending a hand.

She smiled as though she was laughing inside at his formality, but she shook his hand.

She didn't let go.

"We still have tonight, though," she reminded him, and his heart began to race. He wanted to kiss her but didn't know if it was the right time. He had never been intimate with a real woman. He had ordered synthetic relief aids to his room, and while they acted and felt like real people, it was simply masturbation.

This moment was different. His mouth was dry, and he couldn't think of anything to say to her.

"Tell me about your grandmother," she suggested, still holding his hand.

Moss was so lost in her touch that he struggled to think. "She's strong, like you, but also very different. Not that all women have to be similar, that's not what I'm saying. I don't know what I'm saying."

She took a sip, seemingly to cover her amusement. "What else?" she asked.

"She was in the wars, apparently as some kind of commander. She was feared and helped turn the tide. She's brazen, and no-nonsense. Beyond that, I guess I'll have to find out."

"I see her strength in you," Irene said, dropping her hand from his hand to his knee. Waves of emotions surged through him. "Where is she now?" Irene asked.

Moss thought he shrugged, but his body was numb, and he wasn't sure. "I don't know. Seti made it sound like she's in trouble. It's part of the reason I have to get back. You said tonight was the last night. You think Baz will be able to get me out tomorrow?"

"She has many ships leaving all the time," Irene said, eyes downcast. "I'm certain you will be able to leave on the morrow."

"I can't get over the way you two speak," Moss told her, all his energy focused on her warm hand upon his knee.

Irene smiled. "We are a dying breed."

"You may be extinct," he said, feeling as if there was nothing between his mind and his mouth.

She nodded. "We may be."

"We all may be soon," Moss couldn't help but say.

"Better not to think that way," she said and scrunched her face in a false admonishment.

He didn't want to let the moment pass, but he was drained, and she made him nervous. "I suppose I should get some rest."

"Oh," she said, obviously surprised. She regained herself quickly and looked at him with one corner of her mouth upturned. "Shall I accompany you upstairs? With your arm in that sling, you may need some assistance."

There it was.

Moss felt as though he could vibrate off the face of the earth. He knew nothing of women, but the hand, the hungry look she gave him, and the question were enough to make him finally understand.

"Sure, and maybe I could help you out of those as well." He unfurled one finger from around his glass to point at her clothes. His own words astonished him, and he instantly wanted to try and take them back.

Irene smiled a full smile and raised her eyebrows. "I thought you'd never ask."

She gulped down her drink and took his hand, guiding him upstairs to his room.

Pulling him through the door, she kicked it closed behind them and enveloped him in a kiss. The taste of sweat and champagne mingled as their mouths poured over each other.

Moss had kissed girls before, but it had never been like this. It always felt as though they were counting down to stopping and would end with them pulling away and telling him how much they liked him before leaving him to sit alone in his hex, wondering where it had gone wrong.

This was different.

Her hands moved over his chest and through his hair as he gripped the back of her neck, her warm flesh exciting every part of him. It was a passion he had never experienced before.

He kissed down her neck and heard her breath catch, that slight moment making him more excited than anything in his life to that point.

He kept moving, pulling down her top to reveal pink nipples which he began to kiss as a quiet moan left her lips.

She helped him out of the sling she had fashioned, and he wished more than anything that he had full use of the arm. Quickly, she unbuttoned his shirt and pulled it free before running her hands over his well-toned stomach.

As she pulled his pants down, his erection sprang from the fabric within centimeters of her face. She looked up as he stepped out of his clothes.

"This morning all over again," she said with a little smirk.

He flushed and pawed at her skirt with his good hand. She smiled and pushed him on to the bed, giving him another kiss before stepping away and beginning to untie her skirt.

She never broke eye contact, her look inviting him to enjoy as she undressed.

He did.

He could feel his whole body tingle as she pulled pieces of fabric loose.

Her porcelain skin seemed to glow in the dim light of the room, and she clearly enjoyed the effect the swaying of her slight frame had on Moss. He was surprised to see that she was hairless as she pulled her undergarments down.

He had never thought to shave or trim and became very self-conscious of his own hair. The thought passed quickly as she straddled him and pushed him down to the bed with delicate hands. She slid over him, sending ripples of pleasure through his body.

LAYING NEXT to him in the flickering light, hair matted and face glistening, he simply stared at her. He couldn't help but look at the scars.

She noticed, whispering, "I keep them as a reminder."

His curiosity piqued, he asked, "Of what?"

"Mistakes," she said simply.

"You want to be reminded of your mistakes?" he asked.

"Yes, so I may learn from them," she explained. "Our first mission went belly up rather quickly, and I never want to forget."

Moss thought about his own errors. The things he had done and the people he had seen killed. Though he understood the desire to learn, he had no interest in dwelling on what had happened.

"They help me not to repeat," she trailed off. "Do they... am I less beautiful?"

The question caught Moss off guard. "Oh, no. You're incredible."

"You *would* be inclined to say that now."

He stifled a laugh. "Pretty sure I would have said it *before* if it wasn't true."

She smiled. "I suppose that is true."

Moss wanted to keep talking, to enjoy this moment as long as he could, but the day had been full and long, and exhaustion got the better of him.

. . .

THE SOUND of ringing filled his ears before his eyes opened.

The white fluorescent light filled his vision.

"This fucking program," he cursed as he sat up in his hex. He could not access it when he wanted to, and now, here he was, back inside without a clue how he got here or how conscious he was.

His father was nowhere to be seen as he looked around the room. Standing easily, he walked over to his console to see that it was calling someone.

He sat and waited, wondering what his mind (which he seemed to have no control over) had in store for him. He wanted to punch his brain when the screen fired to life, a familiar face looking back at him.

"Moss?" Issy wailed as her big brown eyes filled with tears. "Are you okay? They told me Carcer got you. I've been worried sick. I can't stop thinking about you. Are you okay?"

Moss couldn't believe it. He felt betrayed by his own mind. He had been so happy with Irene but, seeing Issy, all his old feelings for her returned.

"I'm okay," he told her. "I got away. How did you hear about me?"

Tears streaked her cheeks as she choked out words. "Gibbs came to see me. Told me everything that happened, what you did and about your friend Stan. I'm so sorry, but I'm so happy to see you. Where are you? How did you escape?"

Moss shook his head, his mind swimming. He found himself saying, "It's really good to see you, Issy."

"I want to see you in person," she said, and his heart swelled at the truth in her words. "When are you coming home?"

"Soon. I'm trying desperately," he said, but stopped. He didn't know if this was real. His talk with Seti from inside the

Carcer facility had been real, he knew that, but he wasn't sure if he was in a dream. He also wasn't sure why he had called her of all people.

"Issy," he said, and she looked at him with puzzlement. "Tell me something I couldn't know."

"What do you mean?" she asked, sounding genuinely perplexed.

"Just tell me something about yourself, your day, something that I couldn't know," he said, sounding frantic.

"Do you have time for this? What's going on?" She was nervous.

"Please," Moss begged.

She looked away for a moment, seeming lost in thought. "Okay. I was eating at this little Korean place by my house last night, and I had a rubber band in my rice. When I told the waiter, he screamed at me that I planted it there and demanded that I pay before throwing me out. I mean, can you believe that shit? We would never do that at the restaurant. The fucking gall of some people, right?"

She looked at him then as though she was only then remembering the circumstances. He couldn't help but enjoy the little moment, how easy it was for them to slip back into the easy banter of lifelong friendship.

He smiled a moment then nodded. "Okay," he said, before realizing that it really didn't help without some way to confirm the story. He had to do something.

"When did you last hear from Gibbs?" he asked.

Issy looked at him as though she wanted to say something, but answered, "A while ago, maybe a week?"

"Oh, okay," Moss said. Seti had told him they were in trouble recently, so the answer was unsurprising. "Were you going to say something?"

She looked away sheepishly. "Just, oh, I don't know. I'm just happy to see you."

Moss smiled. "Me too. I'm really trying to come home, but I'm in Africa."

Her eyes lit up, then turned worried. "Africa? But you're safe?"

He laughed. "As safe as I'll ever be," he admitted. "Not that it's saying much."

She gave a sad smile. "Seen any animals?"

The question made him happy. He again felt the ease with her that could only come from speaking with someone who really knew him.

"Not really," he said, wondering once more why he had called her. He knew that there was a reason more than just for comfort.

He saw the logo like a flash in his mind. The faint suggestion of familiarity as they were escaping the Safaris.

"Issy!" he exclaimed. "Does ThutoCo have a presence in Cape City?" he asked excitedly.

This had to be it.

She was a former BurbSec officer and might know something he didn't. That had to be why he had called her.

She furrowed her brows. "Moss, what's going on? You're all over the place."

"I know," Moss said, his mind racing. "A lot has happened." "Well, isn't that the understatement of the century?" Issy laughed.

He smiled, wishing more than anything that he was with her. "Yeah," was all he said.

"And I think yes," Issy said, looking as if she was searching her memory. "In fact."

Moss felt his body shake and saw black.

"Issy?" he heard. Not a distant echo but in his ears.

Then a laugh. "Suppose that's the girl back home?" Irene asked.

"What?" Moss said, his mind taking a moment to catch up.

"You were muttering and shaking so I roused you," Irene said.

"Oh," Moss said, hearing the disappointment in his voice. "Sorry for what I said."

"Not a bother," Irene assured him. "It's been a trying day for us all. I was simply worried about you. Was it the program acting up?"

Moss, his trust shaken, lied, "No, just a bad dream."

She had asked a lot about the program. The fact that he thought he had seen ThutoCo logo and had Issy confirm that the company was here made him nervous, despite Irene and Puck's assurances. Seti had said he could trust them, and they *had* both freed him and arranged for his escape, but the fear lingered.

"I'm going to try and get some more rest. I'm sure it's going to be another full day tomorrow," Moss said, turning away and closing his eyes.

"I'll be here," Irene said sweetly, and he hated himself for doubting her.

Pressing his eyes closed, he tried to get back. He wanted to finish talking to Issy He saw flashes of his hex like a computer screen on the fritz, but he couldn't get there.

CHAPTER 8

A small wall clock chimed and Moss groaned.

Glancing around, he saw that Irene was gone, the side of the bed which she had occupied now pulled just-so.

Once dressed and downstairs, Puck looked up from his tea and said, "Toad in the hole?"

Moss blanched, figuring it to be some kind of euphemism. "What?"

"I believe you mean to say, 'pardon?'" Puck corrected.

Moss snorted. "I think, 'what's' fine."

"'Twas an offer of breakfast," Puck clarified with a grin that suggested he understood Moss's confusion.

"Spot of tea?" Irene offered from behind Moss, startling him.

"Sure," Moss said, "though I'm pretty sure I don't want frog for breakfast."

The two laughed, obviously at him. "It's egg on toast," Irene explained.

Moss shot Puck a withering look. "Couldn't you have just said *that*?"

"Sorry old chap, having a bit of fun at your expense," Puck said with a broad grin. Moss sighed his annoyance but Puck, unphased, continued, "Interestingly, the egg upon toast is actually the western version of the dish. In traditional English cooking toad in the hole is a sausage dish cooked in the oven with," and he continued at great length with Moss hardly listening.

ONCE THEY HAD EATEN and drunk, Moss set his plate down and asked, "Now, you two are sure ThutoCo has no presence here?"

There were none of the sidelong glances or shifty looks he had expected. They both simply looked on him with surprise.

"As I said, the family rift was deep," Puck reiterated. "Ask Seti and she can confirm, were your doubts to linger."

Moss looked at them nonplussed. He didn't know what to make of the answer.

"Why do you ask?" Irene asked to fill the silence.

Once again, despite himself, he lied. "No reason, just nervous about them trying to get me again."

Puck nodded gravely. "I will inform you that I have heard tell that Carcer has been sniffing around rather a lot."

"Oh," Moss said, wringing his hands nervously.

"Not to fear, though, as Baz has informed us that she has transit for you this very day!" Puck declared.

Moss sighed. "Good."

He heard Irene make a little sound and he turned to see her covering disappointment.

"Not, not that our time together hasn't been wonderful," he amended, feeling as if it was too little too late. "When will we leave?"

Puck clapped and stood. "Presently, if you are prepared?"

Moss smiled, unable to shake the feeling of accepting a quest in a video game. "I'm ready," he told them.

"Right," Puck said, making for the door. "We shall get kitted and depart."

As Irene turned to leave, Moss moved to put a hand on her arm. She turned beautiful eyes on him, and for a moment, he didn't want to leave. "It was really nice meeting you," he said, unable to think of something more eloquent.

She smiled, though her eyes looked sad. "And you," she said, reaching up and putting a hand on his cheek. "You will be missed."

"Thank you," Moss choked out, overcome with misery at leaving her.

"Just keep trying to save the world," she told him.

He smiled. "Always."

THE DAY WAS EVEN hotter than the previous, and Moss found himself panting as they walked. Puck, even with all his layers, hardly seemed to break a sweat.

"Hot as the dickens, eh?" Puck chuckled, seeing the state he was in.

"I seriously don't know how you do it," Moss told him. "Then again, I haven't experienced any weather for most of my life."

"A sheltered life is no life at all," Puck said with a smirk that implied that he found himself to be tremendously philosophical.

Moss smiled at a memory. "My father always used to say, 'There are two types of people: those who find reasons to do things and those who find excuses not to.' I haven't thought about that in years, but knowing what I do now, I understand it."

"Wise words," Irene agreed.

"Mine was better," Puck frowned, opening his satchel briefly to check the specimen case.

Irene smirked and said in a patronizing voice, "You're very wise."

Puck huffed.

As annoying as Moss found him, he realized he would miss Puck too. Though the man was obnoxious and got under Moss's skin, he was kind and dedicated to his beliefs. Moss felt bad for all the times he had snapped at Puck in the brief time they had been acquainted and made a note to say something before departing. Though he might miss them, Moss was ready to leave, ready to be done always looking over his shoulder and fearing capture every minute. He knew he was being hunted in BA City also, but it was his home and he felt much safer there.

His eyes went wide, and he deviated from their path, turning to look down into a large pit.

"What. Is. This?" he asked in astonishment, watching as people with skin blistering red in the sun sat atop massive gray animals that he recognized instantly from the wildlife videos he watched as a child.

"The elephant rides?" Irene asked, her amused tone entirely lost on Moss.

"They're incredible," Moss stared as one trumpeted, shaking the earth as it moved. Locals with long hooked sticks walked beside the creatures as the riders squealed with delight and took pictures of themselves.

"Had we the time—" Puck began, but Moss held up a hand.

"No, it's okay, I just . . ." he stammered, watching as an elephant wrapped a bushel of grass with her trunk and moved it to its mouth. "I just want to watch for a second."

"A second, we have," Puck offered graciously but with a hint of impatience.

Moss marveled a moment, excited to tell Issy what he had seen.

He often joked with his friends about the way people took

pictures of everything, preferring to share a moment online rather than living it, but now, he wished he could capture the image before him.

"Don't want to miss your flight," Irene noted, and Moss began to walk, watching the animals until the three of them turned and they were again surrounded by humans and buildings.

They stepped off the dirt onto a long asphalt road with blurred waves of heat emanating off it. Cinderblock structures topped with roofs of tarps, stitched bags, and ancient signage lined the roadsides as the people within yelled offers of fruit, water, batteries, trinkets, and various sundries to the passing cars. A drudge that appeared to be more rust than metal was pushing an old jalopy along the side of the road, and several dogs lay panting in whatever shade they could find.

Moss stopped and looked at a stall with a cloth countertop covered in carved acacia wood figurines. Puck folded his arms and tapped his foot with dramatic impatience. Irene stood behind Moss, watching as he picked up one of the figurines.

"You want that?" she offered.

Moss nodded and Irene produced a chip, which the vendor scanned quickly, bowing and thanking them profusely.

"Thanks," Moss said as he tucked the slight object into his pocket.

"A pleasure," Irene assured him. "But we really must."

"Right," Moss said, and they walked at a hurried pace toward a large platform structure set behind a wall of which the cement façade was coated in broken glass. A small piece of fabric caught on a piece of beer bottle danced in the slight breeze.

A guard stood at the rolling metal gate, hiding in the shade of a ripped umbrella. He wore military-style fatigues with tall black boots and clicked his finger against a Bustard-brand beam rifle slung over his shoulder.

"Welcome to Art's Import and Export. State your business," he demanded, drunk with his petty power.

Puck puffed himself up. "Baz sent us."

"Alright." The guard nodded before pressing his ear and speaking another language. "In you get," he commanded them as he turned on his heels and began sliding open the gate.

Puck turned to Moss and extended a hand. "Victoria, if you please?"

Moss's eyes narrowed. "Mind if I keep her? I feel naked without a weapon," he protested, the hairs on the back of his neck standing on edge.

Puck laughed at what he was about to say. "Well, unlike my sister, I have no desire to see you naked. You will send her back to me then?"

"Sure," Moss nodded, finding himself gripping the weapon.

"I hope I can trust you," Puck said with a wink, and Moss felt himself feeling the same way as they walked into the open space with the metal platform at the center. People milled about with packages and dollies, and a pristine-looking ship sat dormant on the platform. The ship was of sleek chrome with black tinted windows, reflecting the sky and glinting in the light.

Moss felt his heart pounding as the door to the ship dropped open. He held Victoria tight as the three of them stood at the base of the stairs to the platform.

Moss exhaled as though he was breathing for the first time when a wide, shabby-looking pilot stepped out. He wore a tattered maroon flight suit with a leather cap with breathing apparatus clipped at one side. His fingers poked out of the tips of his gloves and he scratched at his shoulder absently as he looked at Moss.

"This him?" he asked in a gruff voice. "Assume you got something for me?"

"Here," Puck said, reaching into his satchel and pulling out the case. He held it out.

The pilot took a step forward.

A gunshot reverberated through the space, and the pilot's chest exploded as he was propelled down the stairs.

Moss pulled Victoria out quickly but felt his hand crack as Irene pulled the weapon free.

"You sold me out!" he shrieked in betrayal and agony. He had been nervous and leery of them, but he had hoped desperately that his fears were unfounded. Now realized, he hated them.

"I'm afraid it's far worse than that," a familiar voice said as Ichika stepped through the mist of the pilot's blood which hung in the air, coating her in a crimson sheen.

Moss turned to see Puck frozen in time, his hand extended, not trembling with the weight of the case.

He understood.

MOSS HAD BEEN nervous the first time he ordered a relief aid to his hex. Gibbs had assured him that having sex with a robot would be fun, and no one would know, and even if they did, they wouldn't judge him. It was common, if not openly discussed, and ThutoCo provided the human-looking machines to their employees (at cost) because it was a natural thing to want.

It had taken months of nights scrolling through preferences before he finally pressed ORDER. After watching the money from his account drain away, he paced about his hex nervously. He tried turning on his screen as a distraction, logging into a VR feed of his favorite reality competition cooking show, but nothing could hold his attention as he waited.

His hands trembled as he opened the door for the statuesque blonde with unnaturally large breasts and tiny waist. He ushered her in quickly, checking the hallway to make sure no one had seen her.

No one had.

"Good evening, Employee Moss," the machine said naturally, though the words were stilted. He stood in wonderment of how lifelike she was, how real despite what he knew her to be.

"Hi," Moss said with a little, awkward wave.

She pulled at the hem of her tight red dress and draped herself on the couch. "I'm Sonya. How may I pleasure you today?"

The word "pleasure" sent a shockwave through him.

"We, um, I'm, I think, I mean, I want to have sex," he stammered, averting his eyes and shifting his feet.

"I would like that," she said, oozing sexuality with every word. As Moss understood it, the machines had a robust vocabulary but could not carry a conversation long.

Gibbs had laughed as he explained, "You're not renting them for conversation."

"Would you like me to undress for you?" Sonya asked. "Or I could undress you? Or you me?"

He felt as if he was selecting from a digital menu.

"Oh, sure, okay, why don't you undress?" he said, and she did so easily, not moving from the couch. Once the dress was on the floor, she splayed out for him, and while he found the pose to be a little vulgar, he wasted no time in mounting her.

He finished quickly and, though he had thoroughly enjoyed himself, felt instant shame and wanted her out of his hex so he could shower and forget all about it.

He stood, sticky towel in his hand and said, "Okay."

"Thanks," she said, standing. "That was fu... fu... fu..."

He watched in horror as she repeated the half-word a few more times before stopping, standing as still as a mannequin. He walked over and poked her, and she didn't move.

The speaker in his hex crackled. "Hey, sorry pal. I'm getting a reading that we are experiencing some technical difficulties with the RA in your place. Finish whatever you're doing, and we'll send a tech to retrieve it."

It would be another year before he worked up the nerve to hire a relief aid again, and that one, too, did not work out as he had hoped.

SEEING PUCK FROZEN, Moss knew.

"He doesn't know anything," Irene said as Ichika strode down toward them. "I don't think he's a good enough liar and wouldn't have tried to deceive me."

Moss turned on her with loathing.

"I know, I watched your feed," Ichika said. "That'll be all."

Irene froze too, unblinking in the bright light of day. Her hair wafted against her still face. He reached and tried to pull the weapon free, but the android's hand was a vice.

"Sad, really," Ichika mocked as she descended the stairs.

Moss hung his head.

He was caught.

Again.

He had been caught this whole time.

On all sides, the nondescript workers were now pointing weapons.

"How?" he asked, looking at the woman he had seen killed. He presumed that she, too, had been a copy with her personality mapped into a machine, but he wanted to hear her say it.

She chuckled. "You and your little friends did some good damage, even stopped our ability to do what we wanted on a large scale, but we aren't fools."

"The moment ThutoCo discovered your father was in bed with the enemy, we transferred his research to other labs as well.

Only an idiot would keep all their eggs in one basket, as they say."

Moss realized he was the fool. He had assumed destroying the lab and the servers had been enough. It hadn't been and now his father's technology was being bastardized and used against the very thing which he had been fighting for.

She seemed to read his thoughts. "While you were able to slow us down, you obviously couldn't stop us."

He hated ThutoCo. Hated her. Hated the machines standing beside him and, despite his better judgment, he charged toward Ichika. She dodged him easily and punched the side of his head, forcing him to the hard metal steps. Pain coursed through him as his shoulder hit the stairs. He winced, sucking the burning air into his lungs.

"Why?" he asked, coughing and tasting blood.

Ichika knelt, getting in close. "We are a smart company. Rather than trying to beat the information out of you like Carcer, we thought you might give it up to someone you trust. Your new friends kill me and drop their panties, we knew you would give us what we wanted."

She reached out and patted Moss on the head. "And you did," she said with a wicked smile.

He knew he had. He had told them he didn't know how to work the program in his mind. His heart sank as he realized how easily he was played.

Ichika was right about all of it.
Even having seen the logo and talked with Issy, he had taken them at their word.

He had learned nothing from Grimy's betrayal and was paying for it now.

Despite everything that was happening and the grim reality that he was caught once more, he hated himself for another reason: he had slept with a relief aid once again. He had convinced himself it was the real thing and bought into the moment so easily. He had known Irene for such a short time, yet he had thought they had a connection. Instead, he had been fooled by a machine created with his own father's technology.

His stomach churned. His face burned.

In some cage somewhere, the real Puck and Irene were being questioned, poked, prodded, and having their personalities stolen, all to trick Moss.

He wanted to curl up in a ball and hide from the world. He felt like a poison, a disease that infected anyone he came in contact with.

He forced that thought from his mind as Ichika flipped him over, jammed a knee in his back, and bound his hands.

He tried to remind himself that it wasn't him, it was them. These companies are more concerned with their bottom line than with the people of the planet.

One of Ichika's men dragged Moss onto the ship and threw him into a seat. He didn't fight it, knowing he was caught.

The engine whirred to life and the ship trembled.

He wanted to spit. Wanted to thrash. Something. Anything.

He took a deep breath and pressed his eyes closed.

CHAPTER 9

Moss had no idea how much time had passed, but it felt like a blink.

He sprinted across his hex, taking no time to revel in his new ability. At the screen, he reached out and heard a ring.

He didn't know if this was real.

He didn't know what was real anymore.

But then, "Moss!?"

Even in the program, his body erupted in goosebumps at the sound of Gibbs's voice.

"Gibbs!" he shrieked into the blank screen.

"Moss, where are you?" Gibbs asked. "I can barely hear you."

Moss felt a sharp pain on his face and knew he had little time. Ichika was, no doubt, abusing his body in the real world to pull him out.

"I'm in Cape City, but ThutoCo has me on a ship. I don't know where they plan to take me. Where are you guys?" he asked desperately, knowing it would take a long time for them to reach him and that ThutoCo would have him well hidden by the time they arrived.

"We're here!" Gibbs said jubilantly. "Seti said you reached out but went dark, so we came to find you, and when Issy confirmed, we knew we were on the right track."

Moss had never been so happy in his life.

Though he realized the Seti he had spoken to at Puck's place had been a construct, the program in his mind worked, and now he could make it work.

"Gibbs, the ship is—" he began but his body ripped him from the program as he was punched in the kidney. He saw flickering lights in the ship, people and swaying nets.

Those fucking machines got it wrong; we must get out of here, now! He heard Ichika's neural command.

The ship lurched and ascended quickly.

Moss's face burned as he felt the pain they had done to his body. One eye was already beginning to swell shut. He felt blood pour from his mouth down his chin, and his head rolled as the ship banked. He felt as though he might lose consciousness.

The world around Moss faded as seatbelts and gear crashed throughout the space. He heard angry exclamations from the guards that he could not make out.

Reading ships on radar, but none outside normal traffic flow, a voice Moss took to be the captain's informed Ichika.

Just get us out of here! Ichika ordered. *Who knows what he did in there?*

Aye, aye, and the ship accelerated.

Moss desperately tried to reenter the program, but he was too disoriented and nauseated. He still doubted that the program was even real, though he knew he had spoken to the real Seti once since she had dispatched the fake Puck and Irene.

His mind swam.

He felt the contents of his stomach burn his throat before he sprayed blood, bile, and vomit from his mouth. He gagged and coughed and heard one of the guards scream, "Son of a bitch!"

His body was so wrought that he didn't even feel the baton strike his head, he simply saw black.

A GUNSHOT RANG out in the tiny space and Moss cracked one eye, seeing blurred chaos and fire. Smoke filled his lungs, and he hacked out a cough. He heard more gunfire and shouts and saw a red line moving up the wall of the vehicle.

He didn't feel as though they were moving anymore but could not be sure.

He heard a thud as one of the guards rocketed back in a plume of blood, crashing into the wall next to him. The guard's weapon fell at Moss's feet, and he reached instinctively before feeling the restraints stop his hands. He saw more movement but couldn't tell how many people were in the small space with him.

Crash.

Light.

Moss blinked against the brightness which filled the space and pressed one ear against his shoulder while the blast of more gunfire echoed violently in the confined space.

"Jenkins!" he heard Ichika call out as another body fell at his feet.

Moss heard one word and smiled painfully. "Cunt!" his grandmother called out and through the haze, Moss saw the real Ichika fall dead, grasping the knife in her throat. Sandra knelt and pulled the knife, blood pouring onto the floor as she looked up at her grandson. A shape moved in front of him.

"I'm Luke," Moss heard Gibbs's voice as his consciousness faded once more. "I'm here to rescue you."

Moss wondered if this was a dream, if he would wake up in some ThutoCo holding facility any minute.

"Moss!" he heard Gibbs call, and he turned his head to see

his friend fill his vision. Pain shot through him as he felt a warm embrace before blackness enveloped him.

MOSS CRACKED AN EYE AND GROANED. He felt no pain and knew he was laying flat somewhere. His hands were free but all he could see was a lightbulb hanging from a cord on a ramshackle ceiling.

"Hey, Gingerbread. Your butt-buddy is awake!" he heard Ynna call.

Moss couldn't help but smile at hearing her voice.

Pink hair entered his field of view as Ynna loomed over him. "Welcome back to the world, Mary Sue," she said with a smile, and Moss heard footfalls as Gibbs entered the room.

"Hey, bud," Gibbs said, unable to restrain his enthusiasm. "When you fell from the ship at Carcer City, I never thought I would see you again."

"Makes two of us," Moss agreed. "I need to stop getting into ships."

Ynna laughed. "No shit."

"Where are we?" Moss asked.

He tried to look around the room, but his vision was only just beginning to properly return. It was clear they were in some small room, somewhere, in hiding.

Gibbs and Ynna seemed to be taking a moment to look at him.

"What?" Moss asked.

Ynna snorted a laugh. "Only *you* would have survived."

Moss sighed.

"Seriously, man," Gibbs said. "You've got a ten in luck."

"Fucking wish I could get some of that luck," Ynna snarked.

Gibbs smiled and nudged her. "Yeah, I'll bet."

Moss turned to try to see the room again. "So, where are we?"

"Still in Africa," Ynna said. "Your grandmother has a plan for while we are here."

Moss couldn't help but laugh at that. "Of course she does. What is it?"

He saw Gibbs shrug out of the corner of his eye. "No idea, but it will probably include more murder and mayhem than time at the library."

Ynna chuckled. "So, how many groups you pissed off since being here?"

Moss thought about it. "Same old," he told them. "*And* a charming little gang who call themselves "Safaris" and dress like wilderness guides."

Gibbs rolled his eyes. "Lame."

"Man, you really can't go anywhere without pissing off one gang or another," Ynna half-joked.

"Sounds like you guys got into some scrapes yourself," Moss noted.

"Apple doesn't fall far from the tree on that score," Ynna scoffed. "Sandra attracts trouble like it's going out of style."

"Trouble's always had a way of finding me," Moss heard from across the room. He craned his neck and looked, the shape coming into focus as she moved between Gibbs and Ynna. "Give us a moment," she told the two, and they left, Gibbs giving his shoulder a little squeeze before exiting.

"Hey, grandma," Moss said as he stared at her. She looked better than when he had last seen her. She had put on weight and muscle and appeared powerful for her age. Dressed in black, military-style fatigues, a crimson vest, and broad black hat, she reminded him of Burn.

She smiled at him, the expression looking unnatural. "How you holding up, kid?"

"Pretty fucked up, but I'm not feeling anything," he told her.

"You shouldn't," she nodded. "You're on enough painkillers to choke a horse."

"Figured," Moss said. "What's our next move?"

Sandra let out a throaty laugh. "A lot more like me than your father was."

Moss felt an odd pang at the comment. His feelings about all his family members were so confused that he didn't know what to make of her words.

She continued, "First order of business is for you to heal up. We caused a first-rate ruckus getting you, so we'll need to stay deep under for a spell."

"I don't mind that answer," Moss said honestly.

"In a week, there is a big to-do here, and we need front row seats," she said cryptically.

Moss smirked. "There always is."

"Got that right," Sandra affirmed and patted him on the chest.

"There is one thing I want to do first," Moss said, and Sandra cocked her head.

"That right?"

"Yeah," Moss said. "The real versions of the people who freed me are somewhere, and we need to help them."

Sandra's face grew grim. "Probably dead," she said flatly.

"I need to know," Moss said, his voice desperate. "They are good people doing good work out here. They were taken to get to me, and it's Dad's tech they used on them. I can't leave, knowing they are being held."

Her face knotted, seeming displeased at having to add another mission to their agenda. "I'll make no guarantees."

Moss grabbed her hand. "You will. You find out for me," his voice was strong and stern.

He saw the slightest glimmer in her eyes. "Means that much to you, I'll have Seti put her birds to work."

"Thank you," Moss said, letting his head fall back to the hard pillow.

"Also," Sandra said, giving Moss's hand a hard squeeze. "Thanks for coming for me in C City. I know I weren't your only goal but sounds as if you'd have done it either way. Means a whole hell of a lot."

Moss nodded weakly. "We're family."

"That we are. Now rest up," she said more like an order than a request.

He turned, hoping to fall asleep before croaking, "And Grandma?"

She was now just a dark figure in the doorway. "Yes?"

"Can we talk soon? Like, really talk?" he asked, sounding more sheepish than he had expected.

"'Course," she said and disappeared.

THE NEXT TIME MOSS AWOKE, he felt damp and greasy but well enough to stand. Whatever drugs they had given him were working. Sliding his legs down from the bed—that he realized was little more than a mattress on a stack of pallets—he rubbed his face. His cold hands came away damp, and he had felt patchy, wiry hair growing on his face.

He couldn't remember the last time he had shaved. He had taken no note of it before, but now the bristles touching his nose bothered him. He felt around his eye and could tell it was still swollen, though seemingly healing.

He stood and looked for a mirror, but finding none, he simply walked out the door to the small room and into an open space with a piece of roadside sign sitting atop a spool as a table and several closed doors set into the mud walls.

Anders, the former off-world pilot who had helped them reach Carcer City, was sitting on a folding chair and playing solitaire by candlelight.

"Hiya," he said, his eyes flashing up before returning to his cards.

Moss smiled. "Still with us?"

Anders nodded. "Doing good for good pay's a deal I'll always take."

"Happy to hear it," Moss said sincerely. "Not going to ask me how I'm doing?"

Anders looked up incredulously. "Wasn't planning to. Want me to?"

"No, just seems to be the thing to do," Moss noted with a smirk.

"How are you?" Anders asked with a bemused expression.

"Could use the facilities, honestly," Moss told him, feeling a heavy pressure on his bladder.

Anders hooked a thumb at one of the doors. "Bathroom, such as it is, is in there."

When he returned to the room, Moss sat in a chair across from Anders as he shuffled the deck.

"Everyone out? You my babysitter?" Moss asked.

"Sleeping," Anders told him. "It's the middle of the night."

"Oh," Moss said in a whisper.

Anders set down his cards, produced a bottle from under the table, took a swig, and slid it across.

Moss gratefully accepted it. "Thanks."

"Synthetic shit's got nothing on that," Anders observed. "So, what happened to you since C City?"

Moss thought about how to answer the question. So much had happened, and he found himself replying simply, "Some fucked-up shit."

Anders chuckled.

"How about you guys?" Moss asked.

"Some fucked-up shit," Anders nodded. "Sandra hit the ground running once we got to BA."

"Tell me about it," Moss said, and it sounded like a plea.

Anders stared into memory. "Well," he sighed. "It was quite the situation to get away from C City. Ship took a lot of hits, and we barely made it back to BA. Had to abandon my van, but your buddy, Patchwork, made it worth my while."

Moss had to laugh to himself about Anders's constant talk of money since he knew the man was more altruistic than he ever let on.

"Then we had to set up a safe house," Anders continued. "Patchwork went home to his mom the second we landed, and Judy dropped off the face of the earth. Ynna's pretty worried about 'em but is trying to act tough. Sandra is old school, happy to try and run jobs without a breaker, but it's catching up with us. We get back, you'll need to get Patch back in the fold or replace him."

Moss thought about the statement. He knew that Anders was right but also had a new respect for the old ways. Grotesque abominations of technology though they were, the fake Puck and Irene still managed to get things done without reliance on the computers and equipment that was so common.

"Once we got set up, we started trying to figure a way to get to you," Anders said. "But honestly, everyone was tired and drained. Sandra needed time to get right after so many years in prison. Ynna was all tore up about Grimy and Stan, and the fact that Gibbs had killed a man in such a brutal way was obviously weighing on him."

Moss thought about what Anders was saying. "You mean that he felt like he doomed those prisoners by shooting a hole in the windshield?"

Anders nodded.

"It's worse than that," Moss told him. "In order to save me, he had to execute a man point-blank."

"Ah," Anders said. "Makes sense, he's struggling with this life."

Moss nodded. He knew his friend was having a hard time adjusting.

Thinking back to that first night, after meeting Ynna, Gibbs had forced himself on Moss. He had told Moss that he would never survive in the city alone, but it had become clear very quickly that it was all talk. Moss had a killer instinct, but Gibbs was a gentle soul.

He had been so kind to come, a true friend, and Moss wished he could return the favor.

He knew he couldn't.

"What happened next?" Moss asked, eager to hear more.

Anders began laying out cards. "Sandra and I were doing some scouting, met an old contact of hers, and thought we had a lock on your location. Intel was bad, and she and I got into a scrape. Ynna and your pal got to us in time. I don't need to tell you that girl can fight. Got the situation sorted right quick."

Moss saw the familiar glint in Anders's eye when he spoke of Ynna. He didn't like to see it. Ynna and Gibbs seemed to have an undeniable flirtation and Moss wanted something good to happen for Gibbs, though he knew Ynna was her own woman and would do what she wanted.

"Then we heard from Seti and made our way here," Anders concluded.

Moss thought about his conversation in the basement again. "ThutoCo has a construct of her; she's compromised. I used to be able to communicate with her through our neural network but haven't been able to since I was held by Carcer."

Anders flipped a card. "She said you spoke to her."

Moss leaned back in his chair, rubbing the back of his head.

"Yeah, well, I have a program in my chip that. . ." he trailed off. "Honestly, I don't even know."

"Your grandma mentioned something about that." Anders nodded.

Moss chuckled. "She mentioned it briefly before I fell back into C City. I think I was able to access it *because* I knew it existed. But, like I said, I don't really know."

"That's a trip," Anders observed.

Moss cocked his head. "Which part?"

Anders smirked. "Fair question, but I meant that you have some computer part of your brain doing things you can't control. Would freak me the fuck out."

The words landed heavily. Moss had been so preoccupied with trying to work the program that he hadn't stopped to consider the implications of it all.

"You got robot legs too, yes?" Anders asked.

Moss understood where he was leading. "I do."

"It's a lot of machine," he said.

Moss touched his leg. The synthetic skin felt no different from the real thing.

He cringed, remembering the feel of Irene's skin. Her touch. It had been real to him in the moment.

"I don't even. . ." he muttered, but left the words alone, confusion and sadness coursing through him.

"When it gets hard," Anders said, looking up at Moss. "It's important to remember why we do this."

Moss shrugged, his sense of purpose out of reach.

The corner of Anders's mouth turned up. "You remember Amy?"

Moss thought back. "The little girl in The Conservation."

"Right," Anders said. "That little girl has never left that dome. She has never taken a breath of fresh air."

"I'm not sure I have either," Moss noted glumly, realizing he had gone from the recycled air of the burb to the polluted air of the city to the poisonous air of the outside world.

Anders pointed a finger. "Exactly! We do this for them, for you, for all the citizens of this planet who live in one cage or another. For all the people who live behind digital walls because they don't want to see the physical ones. All the people who are bought and paid for by the very companies that made this planet unlivable. They deserve this world back.

"I joined you not because I want some thrill of adventure or to just fill my coffers, but for all the little Amys out there who have never taken a free breath in their lives. What you are doing is good, outright noble, and that's inspiring.

"I wanted to be a part of that, and others will too."

The passion was infectious, and Moss couldn't help but smile.

The moment was short-lived. "But we are so far from that. We are on our heels all the time."

"Sure, we've taken some hits," Anders agreed. "But you've kept lit the match which will spark the revolution of this planet."

"He's right," Sandra said from a dark doorway, and Moss wondered how long she had been listening. "I'll tell you what every true soldier knows: doing what's right requires sacrifice. We will lose a lot, maybe lose everything, but we won't ever lose hope. I was caged and beaten for years but Carcer never robbed me of my resolve. It's why we'll win."

"Anyone else hear the music swell just then?" Gibbs joked from behind Sandra.

Moss smiled at his friend, figuring it must be morning.

"Way to kill the mood," Ynna said and slapped Gibbs on the back of the head as she made her way to the bathroom. "But it's true," she said as she opened the door. "Burn knew it, and so do all these dramatic fuckers."

She closed the door. Moss stood. "Fine," he said and cleared his throat. "Then I want to take this match and light some shit up."

CHAPTER 10

"Still set on saving your friends?" Sandra asked.

Moss snorted. "Not sure I'd call them friends. The real versions don't know me, but yes."

"Alright, that means we've got a lot of irons in the fire and not much time," she said. "You have any leads on how we might find them?"

"No," Moss admitted. "But I know someone who might."

"Tell me," Sandra commanded.

"This woman, Baz, who I think was working with ThutoCo to set me up and buy time to get me to talk. She's guarded by a small army and probably jumped underground after you guys came for me, but if we can find her, she may know something."

"Alright, I'll see if Seti can hook us up with someone to sniff her out," Sandra said.

Anders cleared his throat. "She may be compromised."

"She's our best bet for now and hasn't steered us wrong yet. Once you're geared up, you three can try to get a lock on this Baz while me and Anders start preparations for the next round," Sandra told them.

"And what is the next round?" Moss couldn't help but ask.

Sandra shook her head. "No need for distractions. We'll cross that bridge when we come to it."

Ynna scoffed. "He's a big boy. He can hear two things at once," she said, turning to Moss. "We are going to infiltrate a Carcer gala being held here at the end of the week."

Moss wanted to laugh at the absurdity of the five of them taking the fight to Carcer once more, but he held his tongue and nodded.

"Maybe if we rescue them, Moss's friends will be of some help," Gibbs put in.

Sandra seemed bothered at having to discuss this. "If they are even alive, we'll see what shape they're in. You all get ready and I'll talk with Seti."

As they all dispersed, Sandra walked over to Moss and asked what he knew about Seti. He filled her in on the fake conversations and she listened intently before nodding and leaving him to change.

It wasn't long before Gibbs knocked and peeked his head in.

"You decent?" he asked with a smirk.

Moss nodded, and his friend walked in wearing bulky body armor under a tee-shirt reading, "Get out your melee weapons, we are feeling around."

Moss knew better than to ask what it meant, not interested in hearing a whole story about some dated reference which Gibbs found amusing.

"You're going to be hot in all that," he said.

Gibbs looked down and opened his arms wide. "Better hot than dead."

Moss smiled. "You've got me there."

The moment held briefly as the two enjoyed simply being in the same room together.

Moss's face dropped. "How you holding up?"

Gibbs ran a hand over his face. "Good and bad," he said finally. "You?"

Moss found the brevity of the answer odd, and he stared at his friend. "What was the name of that game we always played with Issy when we were kids?"

"You feeling alright?" Gibbs seemed genuinely concerned at being asked such a random question.

"Just humor me," Moss pressed.

Gibbs rolled his eyes. "Well, when we got bored of Contrite!, you made us play that silly tropical island city builder for a while, but you gave up when Issy got so much better than you."

"She didn't get better! That's not why," Moss argued, the old feelings of jealousy at Issy's skills rushing back in an instant.

"Whatever you say," Gibbs mocked.

Moss was relieved. He hated himself for the doubt but didn't know what was real anymore. He wondered if he would always have lingering doubts about everyone he came in contact with. He hoped more than anything that ThutoCo would not get to Issy.

Gibbs looked at him with worry. "What's up with you?"

"It's," Moss began, grasping for the words. "It's just been a complicated couple of days. I don't know anymore."

He sat down on his mattress. "I've been hacked, saved, unsaved, betrayed. I had sex with another fucking robot. I've had false conversations that I thought were real, genuine conversations I thought were dreams. I'm all turned around and confused. I feel like I'm losing my grip on reality or what real even means anymore."

Gibbs plopped down next to him. "Yeah, a lot of lines are blurred. Or just straight-up gone at this point. But you have people who care about you. Real people. You have your grandma now and the others. And you always have me."

"I know it," Moss said, feeling heartened but guilty that he was complaining to someone he knew to be struggling too.

"You also have Issy," Gibbs reminded him. "I know things are weird with you guys but man, when I told her you were captured by Carcer... I thought she was going to try and take on the whole company herself."

He smiled softly at the memory of it, and Moss felt his heart swell.

Things with Irene had muddied his mind, but his love for Issy never left him. Hearing what she wanted to do for him made him feel as though he could take on Carcer himself. More than that, though, he wanted to speak to her, to see her.

"Thanks for telling me that," Moss whispered.

Gibbs nodded and patted Moss on the back before reaching around his own. "Also brought you this." He produced a King-fisher Dual-Beam Flip and handed it to Moss.

It was a kind gesture, but Moss found himself looking at the weapon with a certain disdain.

"Thank you," he said, hearing the hesitancy in his tone. "For everything, always," he amended.

"I'm really glad to see you, Moss," Gibbs said, and he felt the truth in his friend's words.

Sandra popped her head in the door. "Got a lead, you kids ready?"

"That was fast," Gibbs observed.

Sandra shrugged. "We've got a broad network. And you," she pointed to Moss, "Seti is looking into how she got copied. Says some crews have been running into traps. With your info we may be able to get out in front of some of these things."

Moss looked at her expectantly, hoping for a "good job," which never came.

"Let's go, time's a-wasting," she said, nodding toward the door.

They followed her into the little main room, and she turned

as Ynna sidled up beside them.

"You three are going to meet with oddDuk, an information broker. Just go sit in the red booth at the Kafee Tropies by Michael Smith Pond and she'll find you. Give her this." Sandra threw a cash chip across the room that clicked against Ynna's metal hand. "And she'll give you the information."

"Just like that?" Moss asked. "Isn't everyone and their mother out looking for us?"

"Put a hat on," Sandra suggested.

Moss shifted nervously and his grandmother chuckled. "I'm just busting your balls, kid. We've set up some distractions to keep the companies occupied. We've got a lot of shit to do this week and don't have time to have folks breathing down our necks."

She spoke with such confidence that Moss was inclined to believe her; though, after being caught so many times of late, his nervousness lingered.

"Not sure I understand what you're waiting on, go!" Sandra said, waving a hand toward the door.

They hurried out like children dismissed from class.

Moss followed as Ynna guided them through a long, low tunnel.

"Sandra sent me the location. Doesn't seem too far from here, but we will take alleyways just to be safe," Ynna said over her shoulder.

"We stick out like sore thumbs dressed like this," Moss observed. Ynna was dressed almost like one of the Safaris. She had on khaki shorts, tall giraffe print socks, a button-up shirt tied just below her breasts, and her hair was pulled into a ponytail.

Gibbs nodded. "Maybe we stop quickly and grab something to throw over us?"

Moss agreed. "Definitely. At least we can look like tourists."

"The way you gawk at everything, you always look like a fucking tourist," Ynna mocked.

Moss scoffed. "Can't all be as worldly as you. My daddy didn't take me on trips around the world when I was a kid."

Ynna's steps stuttered just a bit, and she turned to him with a smirk. "Nope, your dad only got us all into this mess."

The words stung. She was right.

Despite himself, he said, "Sorry you're stuck saving the world rather than living on the street."

He felt bad even as the words left his lips. She had saved him and worked with him but her comment about his father had caused him to snap.

"Perhaps you would like to remember we are on the same team here?" Gibbs diffused.

"Sorry, Ynna," Moss told her. "I've just been through a lot."

Ynna said plainly, "We all have."

Moss knew they were all on edge. "I really am grateful."

"We know it," Ynna said, her tone softening.

The tunnel ended with a staircase, the mud crumbling and cracking underfoot as they moved up. Ynna moved a box that covered the hole, and they clambered out into a narrow space between two buildings so bent with age that the sky was not visible.

Moss moved the box back into place, and they squeezed out onto a quiet street. The morning haze smelled of the sea, and a thick fog sat heavily on the city in a thick blanket. A few people milled about, pushing carts and carrying goods.

An old man turned to them and hurried over, standing close and putting his cloth full of knock-off lenscreens close to their faces. The dirty electronics jingled against one another as he aggressively showed them what he had. He spoke rapidly in a language they could not understand.

They all held up their hands and shook their heads until

Ynna yelled, "Fuck off!"

She wheeled around and grabbed the scruff of a kid whose hand Moss didn't even feel in his pocket.

"Nice try," Ynna told the child and reached into his jacket to pull out a cash chip. "Oh, wah wah," she said in mock imitation of a trumpet and pushed the kid lightly.

He was gone in a flash and by the time the moment had passed, so was the old man.

Moss marveled at how quickly everything had happened and how easily Ynna knew what was happening. He watched as she jogged over to two people reading a flickering menu in a restaurant window, their pale skin crimson from too much unaccustomed sun. Moss smiled as she handed the wallet over to the thankful man whose wife clearly scolded him before thanking Ynna as well.

She came back to them with a broad grin. "Weird to be on the other side of that. Robbing tourists used to be my jam."

"Wife seemed none too pleased," Moss said.

Ynna chuckled. "Oh, yeah, she was piiiissed," she said and broke into a scolding impression. "I told you that you needed to get a bag to wear under your clothes. Remember what happened to me in Paris?"

They all laughed.

Ynna pointed down the road. "Pond is just down this way."

She seemed to have a spring in her step now, and they made their way down the street, Moss's eyes darting about the whole time.

THE POND WAS MASSIVE, with a large statue of a man in its center. It was shallow at its edges, and children were playing in the water, laughing and splashing while their caregivers sat on benches, playing on their palmscreens.

They could see the Kafee Tropies on the far side, a large
neon sign flanked with palm trees guiding their way. The restaurant had open walls with tables both inside and out. A canopy
painted to look like palm fronds hung over the tables, shielding
them from the sun trying to poke through the fog. People sat
and sipped at warm beverages as waiters pushed carts of
steaming baked goods to the tables.

"Stop here?" Gibbs asked, pulling Moss's attention to a cart
where a woman was selling colorful wraps of floral and animal
print patterns.

Some were cut in the style of robes, and Gibbs held one up
to Ynna, "I know you hate to cover up, but."

Her face contorted at the comment. "How I dress is none of
your fucking concern." The joy at helping the tourists seemed
instantly gone, and Moss wondered if something had transpired
between the two in his absence.

Gibbs held up his hands defensively. "I'm just saying."

She cut him off. "You aren't 'just saying,' you're 'saying.' And
if how I dress is too immodest for you, you can go back to the
fucking burbs."

Her eyes narrowed as she snatched the robe and pulled it on.

Gibbs hung his head. "I was only joking."

"A joke has to be funny," Ynna snarled. "And the only thing
that's a joke around here is you thinking you can tell me how
to be."

Moss knew he had to ask his friend what had happened. He
could tell Ynna had been on edge this morning, but there was
obviously something more here. "What's going on here?"

"Nothing," Ynna obviously lied.

"We had. . ." Gibbs began, and elbowed him in the ribs to
keep him quiet. It was enough for Moss to understand.

"Let's just buy these and be on our way," he suggested, and
Ynna nodded vigorously.

Moss shot Gibbs a knowing look. His friend shrugged sheepishly and pulled on a robe himself.

Ynna used a loaded credit chip to pay, and they hurried to the restaurant.

A waiter greeted them warmly as they approached.

"We want that booth," Ynna said, pointing a finger.

The waiter looked and shook his head. "It's reserved."

Gibbs smirked and waved his hand slightly. "You will give us that booth."

Ynna rolled her eyes as the waiter looked confused. "No," he said again.

"Oops, I accidentally left this cash chip here, maybe you can find it a good home?" she said with a wink.

The chip was gone in an instant. "You know, that booth just opened up," the waiter told them and scooped up some menu tablets before ushering them forward.

As they passed a cart, the smell of the warm biscuits, croissants, eggs, and sausages filled Moss's nose, and his stomach gurgled. "I could eat," he told them.

"Me too," Gibbs agreed, and Ynna mumbled something inaudible under the din of the patrons.

"Your booth," the waiter said with a wink, sliding the reserved sign into his pocket after setting the menus down.

It was a pleasant morning with only a few clouds dotting the blue sky. The oppressive heat had given way to a cool breeze and birds sang to one another from the trees which flanked the pond.

Moss started scrolling and selecting food to be delivered to him. Gibbs wasted no time in doing the same.

"You know," Ynna told them with a slightly patronizing tone. "We are here to meet with someone, not to have fucking breakfast."

"I'm hungry," Moss shrugged. "When in Rome."

Gibbs chuckled. "You use that phrase, but I do not think it means what you think it means," he said with an accent.

The food was quickly carted over to them and set on the table, and Moss immediately grabbed the coffee placed before him, blowing the steam off the top. He thought about the first time he tried it.

"Judy ran the second you guys got back?" he asked.

Ynna nodded sullenly. "They took it really hard. I mean, a fight right before Stan died. That would be too much for anyone to bear."

"I wish I could have done something for him, saved him," Moss admitted, guilt coating his words.

Ynna shook her head. "Sandra said there was nothing you could have done. This shit happens."

"She's built for this," Moss said. "She's a soldier."

"So are we," Gibbs said in a reassuring voice.

Once again, Moss's friend surprised him. Despite the warning that he was struggling, Gibbs was obviously growing up.

A shape appeared in the corner of Moss's eye and he looked up. A large young woman with dark skin, short pigtails, and small wire-rim, circular sunglasses slid into the booth. Her leather pants made a peculiar sound as she scooted across the seat.

"You Moss?" she asked, looking at Gibbs.

He nodded toward Moss.

She turned her attention to him and held up a single finger, her hand in fingerless gloves. Moss had seen the greeting in movies but had never done it himself.

He tapped his pointer finger against hers.

"Righteous," she smiled. "Heard about the semen. Botch job but badass."

Gibbs smiled in confusion. "What's that, now?"

"Friend took on the man one sample at a time. No good deed and all but lord's work."

"That clarified things not at all," Ynna said with a bemused smirk.

oddDuk's eyes were just covered by the glasses but she faced the three of them seriously. "You are on the path. No, forging the path. No, off the path now, and the little man is awakening."

"We're trying," Moss said, unsure what else to say.

oddDuk shook her head. "More than trying. Doing. And it is known by all. The elephants stir as the mice skitter underfoot."

"But, actually," Gibbs said, raising a hand. "What's this about semen?"

"We stole a high-value specimen from Bovidae Biotechnics —the company which all but runs this city," Moss said plainly.

"Here, it is not the cows who are cattle," oddDuk intoned.

Ynna seemed to be getting impatient and placed the cash chip on the table.

oddDuk picked it up. "And the gods of capitalism rejoiced."

She took the chip and popped it in her mouth, making a show of swallowing the small device.

"Oookay," Ynna said, stifling a laugh.

"You have some information for us?" Moss pressed.

"Ask and ye shall receive," oddDuk said.

Ynna scoffed. "For money."

"The veil isn't free," oddDuk told them.

"Nothing is free," Gibbs noted.

oddDuk nodded. "Quite," she said. "That which hides is unearthed. Nothing stays hidden in so smart a city."

She pointed up and the three craned their necks to see all the cameras mounted everywhere: on streetlights, walls, and even the passing vehicles. Everything was being captured by someone.

Moss had known it was the same in BA but now, being hunted by so many, the reality of it put him ill at ease.

"Here is where your lurker lies," she said and slid a data chip onto the table, picking up a sausage from Moss's plate in a fluid move. She took a bite, the juices squirting down her fingers. Moss wasn't even bothered that she took the food from his plate; he was mostly thinking about how her glove would smell for days.

"Hold up," Gibbs said. "Couldn't we just skip a step and have her look up—" Ynna elbowed him in the ribs.

oddDuk cocked her head. "More information is available to those who seek."

"No, thank you," Moss hissed.

"We're good," Ynna added for good measure. "Pleasure doing business with you."

oddDuk stood. "Business is all that remains."

She left them and Gibbs looked perplexed.

"The fuck?" Ynna said.

Gibbs shook his head. "What?"

"We don't want to raise suspicion by hacking ThutoCo now. We give them a whiff and they may take Puck and Irene even further underground," Moss explained.

Gibbs dropped his head. "Oh, sorry."

"Sometimes I think you're so stupid that I don't know how you don't just fall over more," Ynna chided.

Moss groaned, entirely over this spat between them. "Cut him some slack, he was trying to help."

"What-the-fuck-ever," Ynna said and pointed to the food. "I guess I have to wait for you to finish eating now?"

Moss smiled devilishly. "Don't want to make an assault on a smuggler's den on an empty stomach."

She huffed. "Fine," she said and dramatically snatched a roll from Moss's plate.

CHAPTER 11

B az was hiding out in a small compound not far from where they had set up their safe house. Seti had shown them the layout, and they had quickly formulated a plan to break in. The area was protected by electric fencing, but only a few guards monitored the perimeter. They were well-armed, though no two of them carried the same weapons. They were no doubt local mercenaries who rented their services to the highest bidder.

The guards stood now around a small brick fireplace with a cut panel of chain link for a stovetop. The cooking meat sizzled and dripped into the fire. Dark, aromatic smoke billowed into the darkening sky.

Guards are working hard, Gibbs mocked in their neural network.

Seti had walked Ynna through the process to unlock the network again in Moss's chip. By her own admission, Ynna was not the best breaker, but she could do low-grade hacking in a pinch if she needed to.

Moss had looked at his grandmother as he groused, "I hate that all these programs in my own mind are trapped behind digital barriers."

She had grimaced and announced in front of the group, "I told you we'd talk, but now just ain't the time."

That had shut him down quickly, and the room had fallen silent thereafter.

Get what you pay for with cheap help, Anders observed. *Ready for me to cut the power?*

Do it, Sandra ordered, and after a moment, the buzz of the fence, which they could hear from the alley in which they were hiding, stopped.

Moss peered over the rank-smelling garbage he was hiding behind to see if the guards noticed the sound change.

They did not. One used their augmented arm to flip the patties. Moss couldn't help but think about Puck and Irene and what they would say about such a use of modern technology.

He watched as one of the guards looked down, and Moss squinted to see what was happening as the man seemed to flick at a bug on his shirt. His body appeared to go stiff, and Moss wondered if it was an allergic reaction before the other guards began to do the same.

What the fuck, Gibbs? Hold your fire, Moss heard Sandra scold.

That isn't me, Gibbs informed them as the man with the cybernetic arm went rigid and fell forward onto the open flame. He screamed before whatever had struck him took full effect, and Moss witnessed the man's eyes go wide with fear as he realized he was being cooked alive with no way of stopping it.

Sandra shrieked in his head, *We have to move!*

They all began to converge on the compound as the buzz of dronepacks filled the air above them and the BurbSec Zetas began to land, scanning the perimeter with smoking weapons.

Moss saw one begin to point in their direction just as he heard the crack of Gibbs's rifle. Blood sprayed from the Zeta's neck as his body careened back, the armor striking the ground with a heavy thud. Moss realized then that his friend had become more cold blooded since they were last together.

The shot set the world ablaze as the Zetas immediately opened fire.

Moss pulled his trigger wildly toward them, his bolt striking and sizzling against the fence as he dove behind a dumpster. He peeked out to watch the Zetas take up defensive positions behind barrels and boxes that littered the space in front of the compound.

The door to the building opened a crack, and the Zetas turned to watch as a grenade rolled out. Rubble showered Moss as the building above him shook from the vibration of the explosion. Ynna slammed into the dumpster next to him, eyes fierce and ready for battle.

"Let them kill each other?" Moss asked.

She shook her head. "Can't let ThutoCo get Baz first. We have to move," she shouted over the gunfire.

Moss nodded, looking toward the muzzle flashes in the smoke and dust.

"Cover me," he told her as she readied her weapon. She stuck out an arm and fired a volley, and Moss stood and ran toward the fence, Kingfisher primed.

Realizing they were surrounded, the Zetas seemed to be focused on the building and took no note of Moss leaping up in the air, his robotic legs sending him easily over the fence.

He hadn't used them like this for so long that he landed on his heels and stumbled, landing right next to one of the Zetas, who turned, his posture one of shock.

A bullet whizzed by as the Zeta began to move his weapon. Moss caught it with his left hand and pressed his Kingfisher into the gap in the Zeta's armor at the armpit with his right.

A crackle preceded the convulsions and more Zetas turned

to face them as Moss realized jumping right into the fray may have been a miscalculation.

Another shot rang out as Gibbs took out one more.

Everyone took cover as blood sprayed. The wind gusted and a dark cloud moved in to meld with the fog. Darkness moved like a shadow over the ground as a light rain began to pitter and the wind carried the drops in dueling directions. Moss squinted as Anders and Sandra leaped over the fence from a dumpster they had pushed.

Anders hipshot one Zeta while Sandra rushed forward with a naniteblade, which cut like butter through a helmet, blood cascading as she pulled it out.

The final Zeta turned his weapon and fired at the new arrivals, who ducked behind cover but not before one shot struck Anders in the leg.

Moss aimed his Kingfisher to take a shot, but the Zeta erupted in gunfire as Ynna jumped down from the fence on the other side, her robe blowing open as she shot. Moss couldn't help but think that she looked like an action movie star and wondered what Gibbs was thinking as he watched her.

The rain began to fall harder, immediately saturating the earth while they stood to assess the movement.

The metal door to the building remained closed, and Sandra barked to Ynna, "Keep that covered."

Ynna leveled her SMG at the door as Moss rushed over to Anders.

He grunted, "Non-lethal. It's numb but I'll live."

"Just keep trying to wiggle them toes, and we'll go in without you," Sandra told him, extending a hand. Anders pulled a charge from a satchel and handed it over grudgingly.

"Weapon up, tight on me," Sandra told Moss, and he raised his weapon as they cautiously moved toward the door.

It creaked and everyone stopped dead, weapons raised, rain pirouetting.

Two shaking hands emerged from the crack in the door.

"Don't shoot," a tremulous voice pleaded from within.

Sandra took a step forward. "Come on out and start wagging that tongue."

"Am I safe?" the voice asked.

"Safer than if you keep us waiting," Sandra said, the implicit threat hanging on every word.

The door moved more, and an old man stepped out, his body hunched and aging tattoos covering half his face. His ratty sweatpants and Trust Fund Maggots World Tour tee-shirt hung heavy as they soaked up the rain. The rifle slung over his back looked more like an antique than a functioning weapon. His fingernails were black and his fingers were speckled with calluses. If he had good years, they were long behind him.

"You've come for the woman?" he asked, holding up a hand to shield his eyes. "For the Baz?"

"Yessir," Sandra told him firmly.

The old man moved forward, and Ynna flinched, adjusting her weapon, but Sandra lowered hers.

He closed in on her and said in a low voice, "You can have her. I don't want trouble; I don't want her here. Just please, please don't destroy my workshop."

He nodded as he spoke, suggesting with his movement that Sandra agree with him. "Where is she?"

"I didn't want trouble. We work together sometimes, and now she shows up and demands to hide," the man justified nervously.

Sandra's body language suggested that she was uninterested in his story.

Moss soothed, "It's alright. You didn't do anything wrong,

and we have no interest in your operation. We just want to get to Baz."

"Locked herself in break room in back," the man explained, his tone relaxing but his body beginning to tremble in the cold and wet.

"She armed?" Sandra pressed.

The man nodded, his body beginning to shake.

Moss lowered his weapon and gestured to the door. "Come on inside," he offered, and the man smiled gratefully and turned. A younger man with a similar face to the older, pushed the door open from the inside, his other hand on a pistol. The young man eyed them suspiciously as though he was expecting them to open fire at any moment.

Ynna looked on them with the same mistrust.

A camera with frayed cords pointed down into the small room, and an ancient dog with red, drooping eyelids looked up at them from a pile of tarps it was using as a bed.

Sandra scoffed. "A grenade's no way to make friends."

The old man shot a scathing look at his son, who dropped his head. "Youth of today is rash," the old man scolded.

"Papa, they—" but he couldn't continue his justification as his father slapped him upside the head.

"Ouchy," the youth whined, and Moss realized just how little a threat they presented.

"Break room has a back door," the man explained. "I take you."

In the warmth of the building, steam rose from his clothes as he pulled keys from his pocket and opened a door at the rear of the room. He guided them through a wide hallway lined with wire racks filled with robotic parts on one side and parts of drudges on the other. They turned left to see wide windows looking into workshops where people sat with soldering irons, wrenches and saws, disassembling robotics.

The H-Vac system rumbled above their heads, and the man's posture shifted slightly as they passed a room with a metal table in the center. The table had arm and footholds and was covered in dried blood. The metal door to the room was locked from the outside and bottles of bleach sat in the hallway.

"Oh, fuck no," Ynna said as her eyes fell upon the room, her metallic finger tapping the trigger guard of her gun.

The old man's steps faltered.

"Not our fight," Sandra said loudly enough for the man to hear.

Ynna scowled. "People like this are a blight on the world."

The old man wheeled around. "I'm helping you now!" he said, face flushed. "How I feed my children is none of your concern, woman."

"Cybernetics doesn't make us any less human, you butcher," Ynna hissed, her voice low and threatening.

Sandra grabbed Ynna by the neck and pressed her against the wall. Ynna's eyes went wide with shock and fear. "You shut your fucking mouth," Sandra commanded. "Leave your personal philosophies at the door when we are on a job, or you can go back to the streets of Redwood Point and see if anyone wants to listen to you whine there."

Sandra let her go, and Moss saw a look on Ynna's face like he had never seen before, like a child who was scolded even though they thought they were right.

"Copacetic?" she asked.

Ynna's eyes narrowed as she said, "Yes, ma'am."

Ynna had told Moss that her relationship with Sandra was more difficult and complicated than with Burn, and now he saw the truth of it. Burn was hard but handled the crew with a soft touch, leaving them feeling protected. Sandra seemed more interested in turning them into soldiers who wouldn't require protection.

In that moment though, she scared Moss.

"We good?" Sandra asked the old man.

He shrugged. "Children, what can you do?"

Sandra's lips began to move in answer, but no words came out.

Oppressive silence descended on them as they trooped forward to a door with a plaque that read "Manager," hanging askew on a single nail that seemed poised to fall from the wood at any moment.

Stacks of yellowed papers, file folders, and books about robotics and human anatomy surrounded a computer sitting on a desk. One of the desk's legs had splintered and a drudge's arm had been jammed next to it to keep the desk aloft.

An electromagnetic pulse rifle hung on the wall next to a dart pistol in an open biohazard box. A chill ran down Moss's spine as it dawned on him what this place truly was. Ynna's words had confused him, not fully grasping the fact that they were not simply doing illegal augmentations here, but hunting people with cybernetics and stealing their parts. He had known that knocking out and repurposing drudges was big business, but the idea that they were doing it to people disgusted him too.

Moss shifted uneasily on his enhanced legs and wondered what kind of price they would fetch. Ire rose within him as he thought about what might happen to the people after these monsters were done with them.

Seti's voice in their heads informed them, *The Zetas haven't reported in, and ThutoCo is scrambling back up. I'll misdirect them, but if any of them have a brain, they'll be moving on your position shortly.*

Copy. Gibbs, keep your eyes open, Sandra replied and looked to the man. "We close?" she whispered.

He nodded and his son pushed a bookshelf aside to reveal a crude tunnel chunked out of the wall.

"Two armed bodyguards and her. You will come through the back," he told them in a hushed tone and brought up the security feed on his computer, enlarging the window displaying the break room. The three within were standing nervously, weapons raised to the front door.

"Thank you," Sandra told him and turned to face Moss and Ynna. "Be ready, but we need this bitch alive so don't do anything stupid like."

She looked directly at Ynna as she spoke the last words, and she nodded, looking as though she wanted to punch the old woman.

They crammed into the tunnel in a row, the space hardly wide enough for one. Pieces of earth crumbled as their bodies brushed the walls. It was dark as they progressed, and they had to work hard not to make any noise as they felt their way forward.

A dim light shone through a poster for workplace productivity they had seen on the feed that was used to cover the tunnel entrance. Sandra stopped and lifted her blade awkwardly in the tight space. Ynna and Moss readied their weapons, and Sandra burst through the poster.

She grabbed Baz from the back and held the blade to her throat as Ynna and Moss pointed their weapons. The bodyguards instantly dropped their guns and held their hands aloft.

Baz dropped her hands. "I know when I'm beat."

"Then you're smarter than most," Sandra said.

Baz shrugged, looking over her shoulder. "I am that," she affirmed. She caught Moss's eye. "Some rats survive even when the trap is sprung," she said, and seeing the state of his face, added, "Though perhaps you lost your tail."

"Only rat here is you," Sandra said and pulled the knife closer.

Baz laughed a long, false laugh. "What is it that you want, if not my death?"

"We want to know where Puck and Irene are being held," Moss told her.

Baz let out another shrill laugh. "You think I know?"

"You're connected throughout the city and work with Thuto-Co," Moss said bluntly.

Sandra added, "Play coy again and these organ harvesters can have what's left of you."

"I tell you what I know, and I walk out of here alive?" Baz asked with a smirk.

One of the bodyguards shifted. "We?"

"Yes, *we* walk out of here alive?" she amended.

Sandra nodded. "Sure."

"Then we have a deal, such as it is," Baz stated.

"Such as it is," Sandra parroted, shifting the blade so close as to graze the skin of Baz's neck.

"ThutoCo has many facilities around the city as they have the food market cornered in the west but wish to expand their operations here. Their president also has contacts throughout the city, and it is clear they are trying to make moves," Baz explained.

Sandra snorted loudly through her nose. "If you're stalling so as to get the jump on us, it won't work."

Baz smiled. "I could use a woman of your intuition on my staff."

"I could use a little more information and a lot less gabbing," Sandra's impatience with the situation was clear. They hadn't heard from Seti again but knew their time was tight.

"Fine," Baz acquiesced. "I know they have a genetics lab off Springbok Square where they also have a secret holding facility. It's not public knowledge, but some of my men were on the construction crew and understood what they were putting in."

"Thank you," Sandra said kindly.

Baz let out a sigh. "That's all I know."

"It's all we need," Sandra said and slid the blade across the woman's neck. She had just long enough to realize what was happening before she slumped to the floor.

One of the bodyguards cried out and dropped to the ground, sobbing in terror. The other simply stared on in horror.

Sandra turned to face him. "Let that be a lesson. You run and you tell the others: this is the price of working with *them*."

The man nodded as he gasped for air, his body working hard to keep from passing out.

The breath caught in Moss's lungs as he watched a drop of blood slide down his grandmother's blade and drop, mixing with the earthen floor.

CHAPTER 12

They had been silent for a while as they hustled to back the home base.

Seti held the Zetas off long enough to mask their escape, but they all knew that ThutoCo would be on high alert now. Anders's mobility had returned enough to walk, but he kept a hand on Ynna's shoulder so that he could keep pace.

Everyone seemed lost in thought and the mood felt low.

As they passed a bar with a light flickering "Open," Sandra turned to face them.

"You three head back and come up with a plan for extraction that will meet with my approval," she ordered before turning to Moss. "I need to catch up with my grandson."

The three nodded wearily, and Moss felt a knot in his stomach. He wanted desperately to speak with his grandmother but worried about Ynna's state of mind. She was obviously angry, and Moss didn't think the company of two men who had their own ambitions with her was what she needed now.

They moved off and Sandra put a hand on Moss's back, moving him toward the door to the bar.

Descending a few wooden stairs, bowed and weathered with

age, they entered a dingy room with rusted chairs set at uneven tables. The walls were coated in layers of graffiti promoting local businesses and gangs. Cracked picture frames displaying images of drunken local celebrities lined the wall behind the long plexiglass bar full of neon illuminated bottles. A cadaverous-looking woman lay on the floor next to a spilled drink, pawing at whatever she saw in her VR headset.

A young man in a tattered smock hurried over to them, a crutch under one arm and one pant leg dangling loose. "Greetings, customers," he said and shook his head. "No, not customers, clients? That doesn't sound good either. Friends? Let's go with friends. Greetings, friends. Can I interest you in a Meadow's Harvest?" He dropped his head sheepishly and admitted, "It's all I know how to make."

"You tend bar and only know how to make one drink?" Sandra wearily asked. "Got any beer?"

The kid frowned. "Expecting a shipment this week, but most folks prefer the synth stuff, more bang for the buck, you know?"

"Fine," Sandra grunted. "Two of what you've got."

He smiled and pulled a jug out from under the bar, pouring a surprisingly thick brown liquid into two glasses.

Moss couldn't help but chuckle. "So, when you said, 'know how to make,' you meant?"

A guilty expression crossed his face. "Yeah."

Sandra grabbed one of the glasses and moved to a chair, telling the kid over her shoulder, "We'll pay when we are done."

He looked to Moss. "Your boss is a bit of a—" he began but Moss cut him off.

"My grandma," Moss corrected, and the kid's face flushed with embarrassment.

"Oh, shit, and sorry I said 'shit,' just sorry," he stammered.

Moss smiled and nodded as he turned to join Sandra.

He took a sip and winced as he sat, the drink tasting like

alcoholic mud.

Sandra shook her head. "Still a sight to behold. My little Moss all grown."

Moss wiped the goop from his upper lip. "I can relate to *that*," he said, trying to form the words. "Seeing you alive, seeing the digital version of Dad—it's all so much. I. . . I thought I had lost you."

Sandra smiled almost imperceptibly. "I was lost. Lost to the world. You came for me. In spite of the risk."

Moss couldn't help but think about Stan, the man who lost his life so Moss could rescue her.

She seemed to know his mind. "And you paid. We all paid."

"I never signed up for this," Moss said, the words leaving him like a dying flame.

Sandra looked at him then in a way she hadn't in a long time: that of familial love. "I know," she told him. "I know we all thrust this upon you and that it has been hard and confusing. But I know another thing: I know that you have risen to this better than we expected. You've survived. Thrived, even.

"You didn't simply fight ThutoCo as your father wished, you took the battle to the whole AIC. You've become quite the man, and you've made this old woman proud."

Moss smiled. He had felt so tired and disillusioned, but hearing her words and thinking about what Anders had said filled him with a sense of renewed vigor.

He looked at the woman on the floor, this person whose life was so meaningless that she needed so desperate an escape. He wanted to give the world back to those people and to those who had never taken a free breath.

"Thank you," he said and truly meant it.

"I know you've got questions," his grandma told him. "I'll try my best to answer what I can, but don't expect the moon. I've been locked away a time."

Moss knew that to be the case and while he had so many things he wished to know, there was one thing he was desperate to find out more about. "So, this program," he began, and his grandmother's face wrinkled as she gave a knowing smile.

"Figured," she said and took a slurp of the sludge. "I'll tell you as much as I know, but you may end dissatisfied with the answer."

Moss groused, "Anything is better than the nothing I know now."

"Right, let me give you a little background and explain to you how it shook out. Your father was a kind man. He wanted what was best for you, but also, the larger world. He believed his personality mapping would make drudges more efficient and better to work with for the user. An adaptive AI founded on the mind of the operator could feed more people more quickly.

"He would wax philosophic about how we relied on computer learning too much and tell anyone who would listen that true success would come from machines controlled by people *supported* by computers. He trusted the company and only came to realize what they intended to use his research for when it was too late.

"Your mother was not so naïve. She began to see the forest for the trees much sooner than him, and they would get into epic bouts, going round and round. When your father finally came to see the truth, the walls were already closing in. He knew Burn and I were working to fight the companies for what they did to the veterans, and he explained his idea for the program. We supported the idea but, he feared the company would move before you were old enough to do anything about it, and so we came up with a plan to hide the program until you were grown."

She took another sip. "This is real swill," she observed.

Moss desperately wanted her to continue but let her have the moment as she seemed to be reliving as much as retelling.

"Your dad went to your mom to encrypt the program for you, and she came to me. She explained that if it came to you, it meant they was gone, and you would need every advantage. She broke every corporate policy to make your program as powerful as she could, filling it with all the developed research she could get her hands on, much of it still in testing and all of it, proprietary. I won't pretend to understand any of what's in your chip now, but it's a lot. Much more than even I know.

"She never told your father what she did and swore me to secrecy. Lying to your child ain't easy, but I knew it was for the greater good." She trailed off a moment, eyes sad with the memory. "And better for you."

Her eyes grew wet and she cleared her throat in an attempt to suppress the emotions. Moss realized that for as tough as she was, she carried a lot of guilt beneath the steely demeanor.

"She also passed along another program which would bypass neural privacy settings and allow a user with a ThutoCo implant to hear the thought commands—what Burn gave Ynna in case you needed convincing."

Moss tapped his temple. "Still comes in handy. I can hear the Zetas."

Sandra chuckled. "Yeah, your mom was a pain to play chess with. She could always see the next ten moves."

"I wish I had known her better," Moss said bitterly. "Both of them, really."

"I'm sure they felt the same way," Sandra said, finishing her drink and signaling for another.

The kid hobbled over with the jug and topped her off. "Anything else I can get you?"

Sandra pointed to a pack of cigarettes jutting from a small pocket in his apron. He produced the pack quickly and looked to Moss. "You?"

Moss nodded and the kid slid two out, lighting both.

The two took long drags, and Sandra said, "Your father would kill me."

Moss laughed loudly, smoke billowing from his mouth. "Dad got me involved in far more dangerous shit than this. I mean, I was attacked the moment I got to BA, and it only got more deadly from there!"

"So I've heard," his grandmother told him and took a long moment to examine the embers, turning the cigarette between her thumb and forefinger. "They both loved you so much, you know."

Moss smiled weakly. "I know."

Sandra had a distant look, and a single tear rolled down her cheek as she said, "I've lost a child. All the things I've seen, people eviscerated as they scream for their mothers, dropships on fire, hospitals reduced to rubble, nothing has had such a personal impact as that.

"But to think of your parents, taken screaming from their homes and, in their final moments, knowing they would never see you again."

She trailed off. Considering her words, he felt worse than all the times he had been shot.

Everything he had seen and been through, mixing in his mind with the alcohol and painkillers was too much for him. He wailed and began sobbing, releasing it all in a heaving, blubbering cry.

He felt an arm draped over his shoulder and he clutched his grandmother's hand.

When he could finally speak, he choked out the words, "It's just so much. We go from one thing to the next with hardly a moment to think."

"I know," Sandra soothed, the words sounding awkward. "You alright?"

Moss wiped his face with his sleeve, sniffled and, having let it out, answered genuinely, "Yes."

"Where were we?" she asked, returning to her seat.

Moss chuckled, his brain such a soup that he couldn't even recall.

"Oh," he said. "You told me all about the program but not how it works."

"Cuz I don't know," she admitted.

Moss shook his head. "I was worried you'd say that. I'm guessing Mom didn't leave you an instruction manual?"

"I got arrested, presumed dead; if she did, it wasn't with me," Sandra said as she stubbed out the cigarette on the table. Moss looked down to realize his own had burned out.

"So, what then?" Moss asked.

A single strand of white hair fell in front of Sandra's face and she coiled it around her finger and pulled it out before jamming it in her pocket. "When we finish these next jobs and get back to BA, you practice and try to learn."

It was not the answer Moss was hoping for. He wasn't sure what he wanted, but he knew it wasn't that.

"What else?" Sandra asked.

Still feeling like he was swimming in questions, he grasped at the first one that came to mind. "What was the story with you and Burn? He was always so cagy about it."

"'Fraid I'm gonna be cagy about it too. This trip down memory lane's been tough enough without getting into all that," she said, reminding him of the way Burn had answered the question.

"What happened in Carcer City? We left quite a shit show in our wake." He had wanted to ask Gibbs this, but things had been so strained with Ynna that he had left it.

Sandra snorted. "Nothing really happened. D2E ran coverage vilifying the prisoners, and the guards were given a ten percent raise over the next ten years to shut them up. Where ThutoCo may be a prime example of making slaves of their employees through perks, Carcer is the example of corporate bloat. That company grew so fast during the pandemic that every bad instinct and poor decision was made policy.

"Alice Carcer is the physical embodiment of everything wrong in this world. It's why we're gonna send a message once we get your friends."

"So, it's not personal?" Moss asked. "Punishment for what Carcer did to you?"

"Fuck yes, it's personal!" Sandra barked. "I ain't too proud to admit it, but that's just the icing."

Moss laughed, appreciating the honestly. "And we steal their tech, whatever it is, what then? What's our end game?"

Sandra seemed to puzzle at the question. "We use it to help take down Carcer and ThutoCo and the rest of the AIC, give the planet back to the people."

"You think we can?" Moss asked sincerely.

Sandra shrugged. "I know we can try. Moss, you must under-stand, this planet feeds and supplies all the colonies. There is absurd wealth being funneled back down here, and the people who live here get nothing. It's an obscene misbalance we fix to right."

"Sure," Moss said, "but sometimes. . ." He couldn't find the words.

His grandmother gave him a knowing look. "I understand, you look at people like her." She hooked a thumb at the woman lying on the floor. "And you think, maybe the people don't want the planet, they are content in their own way. But it isn't true. They just don't know, don't understand that things could be different. They've been pawns so long that they don't even see the hands moving the pieces any longer. Those of us who do need to try and do something."

"You're right, I know," Moss told her, and he really meant it. There had been something in him that had wanted to fight for what's right his whole life. He had never fully understood it, but he had known it was there. "What do they want?" Moss found himself asking. "The AIC, I mean. These large companies are all working together toward some end but what is it? They already have a docile populace, but they clearly desire more."

He had been curious about this for a long time. When he had learned that ThutoCo wanted to kill their employees, it had not made sense. He felt like there were less lethal ways to achieve their goals.

Sandra looked at him in a way he could not decipher. "I don't know," she admitted. "You're right, they're doing something we can't pin down.

"That's the other reason we fight. Figure out what they are up to and expose them. We know it's not something altruistic."

Moss agreed. "Of that, there is no doubt."

"Now, I've got questions too, if you're up for it," she said.

He was surprised. His grandmother seemed to know so much, and Moss felt that he had so little to contribute that he had not expected the suggestion.

"Of course," he told her.

"What was it like growing up," she asked quietly. "Once they were gone?"

The question she asked took Moss even more by surprise. "Oh, um, it was fine really. The company provided a hex for me and an education. Though I now realize they taught me only skills applicable to the job, really.

"I had time to go out, and my meals were taken care of, and I just needed to be back in my room for curfew. It was all I had ever known, so it felt like a normal childhood."

"Only thing missing was family," Sandra said, her voice dripping with sadness.

Moss shook his head. "I always had Gibbs and my friend Issy's father was always there for me when I needed him."

She smiled weakly. "That's something, anyway."

Moss saw the heartbreak all over her face. "You were locked up. There was nothing you could have done."

Sandra snorted. "Don't mean I can't regret it."

"Sure," Moss agreed. "But really, I was fine. It made me who I am today, and we couldn't have run the ThutoCo job without Gibbs, Issy, and Vihaan."

"I'll grant you that," she said and turned to look him in the eyes. "And I need to know: Why is rescuing the two locals so important to you? And don't give me that 'No man left behind' answer. I know there is more to it."

Moss had to admit that there was. "It's Dad's tech," he said. "Bastardized and misused. You said yourself that he was designing it with altruistic intentions. To think that it was used to copy some people's personalities against their will is galling.

"Plus, and not for nothing, it was used that way to get to me. The idea of leaving them to suffer any longer on my account feels wrong."

Sandra's face showed that she understood.

Moss scratched at his chin. "Do you think. . ." he began but decided to let it go.

His grandmother's brows raised with curiosity. "What's that?"

"Oh, I don't know, just a thought," Moss hedged.

Sandra grinned at him. "You know I ain't gonna let this go."

Moss grimaced, wishing he hadn't said anything. He decided just to tell her, though it made him nervous. "You said my chip is full of ThutoCo intel and tech. Do you think it's possible for me to use it to break Puck and Irene out without us having to go in?"

"Little tired of guns a-blazing?" she asked and his face flushed. "It's a good notion, and I think you may be on to something, but it'd be all on you. Would be good to test how powerful you really are."

"Yeah," Moss said.

"Bet you're a lot stronger than you know," she said with confidence.

The corner of Moss's mouth turned up. "I hope so. So, maybe we can do this quickly and quietly."

"I'm not one to ignore a good idea," she told him. "You up to try, you'll get no argument from me. We just need a solid plan. And a backup plan."

Moss considered the words. "Maybe if we get close enough, I can use my program to synch with their systems and get them out."

Sandra finished her second glass. "You have enough control over the program to try?"

Moss chuckled at his own expense. "Hardly," he admitted. "The program seems to be controlling me more than the other way around, but I'd like to change that. And who knows, maybe just knowing more about it will help me to control it."

"Worth a shot," Sandra said. "And if it doesn't work, we just go in and kill every corporate motherfucker and grab your friends."

The comment gave him a renewed sense of purpose. Much of his life had been spent as an unwitting cog in the ThutoCo machine, and he wanted to spare people like himself if he could. "Let's see if my way works," Moss said, hoping he could finally do something that he had yet to truly accomplish.

"Alright, let's head back and let 'em know the plan," Sandra said, beginning to stand.

Moss finished his drink, cleared his throat, and said, "Maybe after one more."

He was not yet ready to let the quiet moment with his grandmother conclude.

CHAPTER 13

"She hasn't come back!" Gibbs, wearing a woman's bathrobe, shrieked as Moss and Sandra stepped through the door. Anders lay asleep on the couch with his feet up on an armrest, a dusty hat over his face and a blanket covering his naked body. His wet hair soaked through the tee-shirt being used as a pillowcase, and a pile of damp clothes lay sopping beside him.

"It's alright," Sandra told Gibbs.

He shook his head, face red with consternation. "It's not alright; she could be anywhere."

Sandra let out a low laugh. "We all know where she is."

Gibbs stamped his foot. "You told her that wasn't our fight!"

"At the time, it wasn't," she explained slowly. "But what that girl needs to do in her free time ain't our concern."

"It's dangerous out there!" Gibbs shouted, and Anders snorted before rolling onto his side, the hat rumpling against his face.

Moss couldn't help but laugh. "If anyone can take care of themselves out there, it's Ynna."

Sandra looked at them blankly. "You two take a room, let the pirate sleep, and I'll check in with Seti."

Gibbs did not like the suggestion, and Moss put a hand on his shoulder, turning him and pushing him into one of the adjoining rooms. His friend's back was damp against Moss's palm as they entered.

Moss shut the door and Gibbs wheeled on him. "You smell like cheap booze," he accused.

Moss smiled and shrugged. "I just drank some cheap booze."

Gibbs scowled. "At a time like this, you really think that's wise?"

Moss stifled a laugh, the alcohol coursing through him. "Is anything we do wise?" he quipped.

"Oh, don't pull that on me," Gibbs snarled.

"Come on, sit down," Moss suggested and plopped down on the mattress. He wanted to help his friend calm down. "Tell me what's really going on."

"You know what's really going on!" Gibbs said.

Moss patted the spot beside him. Gibbs sighed and sat.

"I can think of a few things, but I won't know until you tell me," he said sincerely. While he did have several guesses as to what was upsetting his friend, he wanted to hear it.

"It's, well, I don't know," Gibbs said, and it was obvious that there were several things bothering him at once.

"Is it the killing?" Moss suggested. "I know that's been hard for you, and we haven't really talked since Twelve."

"No. I mean, yes, but, no," Gibbs said, sounding as if he wanted Moss to keep talking, but he didn't.

After a moment, Gibbs continued. "That's getting easier. I struggle with it all but seeing Twelve about to kill you left me no choice. And the others, I don't know. They are agents of oppression, happy to put a bullet in me as soon as look at me.

"Doesn't mean I enjoy it, but it's bothering me less," he concluded.

"Still bothering you, though?" Moss asked, figuring he knew the answer.

"Of course," Gibbs said. "Doesn't it bother you?"

"Not really," Moss admitted. "They know what they signed up for, same as us, and if they don't mind hurting me, I don't mind hurting them."

Thoughts of his new plan played in his mind, and he amended, "But I don't want to hurt the little guy who's just doing a job."

"Me neither," Gibbs agreed.

Moss looked into his friend's eyes. "So, if it isn't that, what is it?"

"I just worry about her," he squeaked.

"Even though you know she'll be fine?"

Gibbs nodded. "Logically, yes, I know. But I can't help how I feel."

"You guys fucked, right?" Moss asked.

Gibbs grimaced, looking to the floor and shaking his head. "Why do you have to say it like that?"

Moss chuckled softly. "For someone who's spent his whole adult life bragging about supposed conquests, it's a little odd for you to be so sheepish now."

Gibbs rubbed his face with his palms. "You know as well as I that that was all talk."

Moss did, of course, know that, but he never expected Gibbs to admit it. "So," Moss lead.

A long silence followed. Gibbs shifted uncomfortably, lost in thought.

"Yeah, we hooked up," he finally said. "It was really wonderful, but I think I ruined it all by liking her too much, and now things are so weird."

Moss smiled sweetly. "I'm happy and sad for you."

Gibbs rolled his head. "Me too," he whispered. "You know, it was my first time with a real girl."

The comment made Moss cringe, and he admitted, "You have me beat. I thought mine was with Irene, but turns out it was just another fucking relief aid."

"Can't get enough of them, eh?" Gibbs joked softly. "Sorry."

"Me too," Moss said. "But Ynna will be fine, and you guys will work out whatever this is between you."

"Thanks," Gibbs said. "Who knew sex could make things this complicated?"

Moss chuckled. "Literally everyone."

"You had sex with Irene," Gibbs began. "What does that mean for you and Issy?"

Moss had been mulling that very question. "It means I need to see her when I get back. This whole thing has put it all in perspective for me, and if I'm going to risk my life daily, I need to tell her how I feel."

"Bravery comes in a lot of different forms, I guess," Gibbs observed.

Moss had to appreciate the wisdom of his friend's words. "Yeah, it's weird that I can pull a trigger more easily than talk to a girl I've known my whole life."

"At least you can pull a trigger," Gibbs self-deprecated.

Moss smiled at his friend. "You're doing great, man. You got thrust into something you weren't even a part of and stepped up. I'd be dead several times if it weren't for you, and you're doing real good by staying with us.

"I understand that none of it has been easy. Shit, I understand that better than anyone, but I couldn't be more proud of you and couldn't have done any of this without you."

Gibbs blushed. "Thanks," he said and smiled. "You've always been a great sidekick."

Moss grinned. "Right."

THE TWO ENTERED the main room to find Sandra looking at a holoprojected schematic of a tiered circular building. Anders still slept, one arm draped over his face. Sandra glanced up at them and beckoned them to approach.

"Your plan just may work, assuming you can actually do what you suppose," she said in a low tone, glancing over to ensure Anders didn't wake. "But it'll be all on you."

"I'm becoming accustomed to that," Moss smirked.

Gibbs looked confused. "What's the new plan?"

"Didn't tell him?" she asked Moss.

"Didn't get around to it," he said.

She gave Moss the slightest wink and turned to Gibbs. "He's going to try and use that program of his to breach their security and get his friends out."

Gibbs threw his hand up. "Of course you are," he shrieked with exasperated exhaustion.

Anders snorted and cracked an eye wearily.

"You'd rather we shoot the place up?" Sandra mocked, and Gibbs turned a bright crimson.

"I don't know what I'd rather," he said and stormed back into his room, slamming the door and causing the wall around the frame to buckle and crack.

Moss sighed, feeling like his whole talk with Gibbs had been in vain.

He turned to his grandmother. "You know you can let some of them go," he said, more tired than angry.

Sandra scoffed. "Burn took it easy on your asses, and that's why y'all fuck up as often as succeed. You're a bunch of kids playing at hero, and I intend to change that."

The woman from the bar was gone and the tough-guy façade was back in full effect.

"Fine," Moss sighed and was about to speak, but Sandra interjected.

"You'll thank me when you're not dead," she said, pointing an accusing finger.

Still warm from the alcohol, he had to stifle a laugh at her theatrically. "I've managed not to die so far." He shrugged.

"You may have my instincts for survival, but that'll only keep you upright so long," she said.

Moss was disinterested in this line of conversation. He felt like he had a nice moment with her just before and that this tough love bit was unnecessary.

Anders groaned. "What's this about a new plan? I don't have to get shot?"

Moss was grateful to the man for cutting the tension.

"We are going to try a different method this time," Moss said.

Anders gave a thumbs-up and got up from the couch. "I've got to piss something fierce, but then I want to hear this new method."

Moss and his grandmother stood in silence as the sound of splashing urine filled the space, the door doing little to dampen the sound.

Moss looked at the grime under his fingernails and thought about the fact that everyone seemed to have to go pee when they were trying to make plans. Anders emerged as Moss pulled some dirt from under his nail with a thumb.

He came over to the schematic and said, "What's this all about?"

Sandra talked them through the plan as she saw it, showing Moss where he would enter and where he would need to go.

Watching her walk him through it, Moss realized just how alone he would be. It was important to him that he do this, try to save Puck and Irene as well as try to actually take control of the program, but it was intimidating. Sneaking into another ThutoCo facility by himself was dangerous and, though he knew he would have backup, they would be outside and would take time to reach him if things went belly up.

He paced nervously as he listened and reached for his weapon when he heard the front door creak.

Ynna strode in through a cloud of cigarette smoke. She was coated in blood splatter but wore a calm expression.

Sandra barely looked up at her. "Feel better?" she asked, but before Ynna could answer, Gibbs burst from the room and ran over to her, embracing her tightly.

Ynna left a crimson handprint on his back as she returned the hug.

"You're alright," Gibbs sighed, looking as though he might cry.

Ynna chuckled sweetly. "I'm fine. Just had to do it."

"Saw something in there you didn't like?" Anders asked, and Moss remembered that he had stayed outside.

"He didn't fill you in?" she asked as she tried to squirm out of Gibbs's arms.

Anders shook his head. "Nah, he was a little worked up."

"I can see that," she said lightly as she pushed Gibbs off her.

Moss was more than a little unnerved that she had gone from so tightly wound to so loose after—he assumed—killing at least two people.

She dropped her cigarette and stamped on the embers with a blood-covered boot. "I was modified before I was even born," she told Anders. "And people who think of the modified as less-than piss me off to no end. But people who slaughter the augmented will get no fucking quarter from me."

Sandra shook her head slowly. "You know someone will just rise to take their place."

Ynna smirked. "Sure," she admitted. "Doesn't mean I can't do some small good for the world."

"Good?" Gibbs repeated.

Ynna smiled wickedly. "Removing evil from the world *is* good."

"Get no argument from me on that score," Sandra said. "So long as it's on your free time."

Ynna ignored the comment. "And those two won't be chopping anyone else up anytime soon. Shoulda seen his eyes as a cybernetic hand he'd love to have sold choked the life out of him."

"Yikes," Moss heard himself mutter.

"Go back to the burb if you don't like the way things work," Ynna said sarcastically but without the heat her comments had in the morning. He was surprised by her. He had known her to be tough and ruthless, but going back to murder those two seemed unusual.

He wanted to ask more questions but knew now was not the time.

"What are we working on now?" she asked, looking at the projection.

"Moss is going to try and grab his friends without killing," Anders told her.

"Great," Ynna said, turning to Moss. "Those fuckers at the chop shop would have loved to crack you open and sell that brain of yours for parts, by the way. So, you're welcome."

He hadn't thought of that. He had been so preoccupied with his robotic legs that he hadn't even considered his chip. "Thanks," he said, the word sounding like a question.

"No problem, half-bot," she said with a wink.

Gibbs put a hand on her shoulder. "Can we talk?"

"Sure," Ynna nodded, and they excused themselves into a side room.

Moss was relieved that they were going to sort out whatever was going on between them.

"Ready to get ready?" Sandra asked Moss.

He nodded.

"Good," she said. "Let's get this sorted so we can heat up the pan to fry up some bigger fish."

CHAPTER 14

M oss hated being fully encased in his Dermidos, feeling both stifled and naked at the same time.

The ground beside him shook as the heavy garbage truck rolled by. He hopped up easily and grabbed the grip, riding invisibly on the side.

He listened as the driver shouted into the speakerphone in the cab. "He's still mine," the driver shouted to be heard over the rumble of the vehicle. Moss could not make out the other side of the conversation. "I've raised him for six years! He's my son no matter who his father is."

The voice on the other side of the call was saying something, and Moss felt guilty hearing so intimate a story.

"It wasn't cheating. We were only just dating at the time," the driver said as the ThutoCo structure came into view. "You and I are very different then," he said as the truck slowed, reversing toward a large garage door. "I won't abandon my boy," the driver yelled over the loud beeps of the truck backing up. It skidded to a stop. "Hold on," the driver said and opened his door, waving a greeting to the BurbSec officer standing beside the control panel to the door.

Though he knew he was cloaked, Moss still jumped down quietly and moved along the side of the truck before ducking and scampering into the garage. The space was relatively small and utterly unadorned. Trash cans full of coffee cups, disposable meals, and shredded paperwork lined one wall, and a locked door with digital keypad sat in the middle of the rear wall, leading into the facility proper.

The driver muttered and coughed as he dragged one can at a time to the truck, the plastic smock that he wore covered in splashed garbage.

Now Moss would wait, his heart thumping against his chest as he stood by the door. It felt odd, like he should be seen simply standing there.

After a moment, the garbage had been wheeled away and the garage door closed slowly, casting Moss into blackness. A motion sensor light would illuminate the space if Moss moved, so he stayed perfectly still after clipping a small electronic device to the wall under the camera.

Moss knew from Issy's time at BurbSec Academy that the cadets were made to check empty rooms periodically on rounds and that eventually, someone would come through. ThutoCo productivity points were based on tracked job performance so the cadets were diligent in their duties. If checking an empty room meant they were one step closer to the next level of employment, they would certainly do it.

He thought about Issy as he waited. Those early days after graduation, speaking ad nauseam about the menial tasks she did throughout the day. He smiled at the memory. Something which had been so boring to him at the time seemed so enjoyable to him now: He would love to sit in his hex and listen to her talk all about her mundane day.

As time passed, he tried to keep from shifting, but it was

uncomfortable to just stand there, so he would occasionally lift one leg or move about a little.

He broke into a cold sweat when he moved too much and set off the light. No one seemed to notice, and no one came into the room, and, after a bit, the light shut back off.

His body tensed when he heard a click and the door slowly opened.

"In here," a hushed voice said and giggled. The light clicked back on, and two young employees in their traditional ThutoCo linens entered eagerly, pawing at one another as they stepped into the space. Moss slid through the door behind them before it clicked closed.

He pressed himself against the wall of the bright fluorescent-lit hallway. Even through the suit he could smell an odor so familiar that it felt like being home. He had always thought of it as freshly opened plastic, but he now knew it was a simple cleaning concoction that ThutoCo used to keep their facilities pristine. It was an odd sensation breaking into a place that felt so familiar.

Remembering the schematics, Moss moved down the long hallways, past doors and frosted glass windows through which he could see the vague shapes of people working. He kept to the walls in case some person darted by; an employee bumping into some unseen force would certainly raise alarms.

He heard the din of a television and knew he was getting close. He inched forward toward an open door and peered into the break room. It was as different from the last one he had been in as could be: rather than a motivational poster and ratty furniture, this room had all the amenities a person could want. Comfortable couches lined the walls, the gaps between filled in with Foodiers, coffee and vending machines, and computer terminals where an employee could make reservations at restaurants, arcades, or local tourist destinations.

A screen mounted in the corner was blaring. Hugh Dean, a popular D2E host was shouting to an assembled audience, "And when life gets to be too much, what do we do?"

He pointed and the crowd roared, "Just don't care!"

Dean clapped and smiled as he paced behind a podium. "You could complain about the same thing all week and not do anything about it or...?"

"Just don't care!" The audience repeated in unison. Moss found the immensely popular mantra sad and disheartening, but he knew it was how many people throughout the world coped with their lives.

The BurbSec cadet seated in a padded chair with her feet up on a table was smiling and nodding along with the program.

Moss knelt slowly, his hand trembling. He was thankful that the television was loud enough to mask the sounds of his movement as he moved slowly toward the keycard dangling from her belt.

"How do I stay so happy when things get hard, I...?" the TV blared.

"Just don't care," the cadet said along with the crowd, causing Moss to flinch.

The clip rattled as he opened it, and he looked up to check that she was still watching the screen.

She was.

He slowly pulled the metal clip off the ring on which it was hung and took a slight breath. He tucked the card in a pocket to keep it cloaked and wanted to dash from the room but knew better. He crept backward on hands and knees, his eyes darting forward and back to ensure he wasn't about to be caught.

Once he was clear of the door, he slumped against the wall, panting. His instincts had carried him through countless fire-fights, but this skulking around was foreign to him. He felt as though he was about to be caught at any moment. The internal mechanisms of his suit were keeping his temperature regulated, but he could feel the sweat pooling under the gloves. The next part would be the riskiest, Moss knew, as he steeled himself and moved toward the control room.

He needed to hack the system from the room, but he knew it would be occupied and that opening the door without the person inside noticing would be tough, if not impossible. As he neared the door, he pushed from his mind the idea that he still didn't know if he could even control the program.

He slid his thumb to bring up a menu displayed inside the lenses of his mask and activated the device he had placed beneath the camera in the garbage room. It would short the camera before dropping to the ground and self-destructing, and Moss hoped that the two people in the room were too busy with one another to notice. Though the device was small, it made him nervous.

He slid the keycard from his pocket and pressed it against the reader, causing it to beep. His heart jackhammered at the sound echoing through the hall. He had to remind himself to breathe. Holding the door slightly ajar, he waited to see if he had aroused any suspicion. When nothing happened, he pushed it open slightly and peered in.

An old, fat man sat at a bank of monitors, slapping one and grumbling to himself. He had thinning hair that he had lathered in jell and forced into position over a bald spot. Hunched over as he was in the seat, tufts of back hair protruded from the gap between the bottom of his shirt and top of his pants.

"Come on," he griped at the distorted image, leaning sideways in his chair to check the cables to the monitor, his furry back facing Moss.

Moss crept in and closed the door softly behind him, sighing with relief before realizing he had another problem. The space was small, with just enough room for the desk and computers but very little for him to hide. If he was able to access the program, he didn't know what his actual body would do in the real world. If he shifted, his legs would kick the chair of the operator.

He wondered if this was even worth the effort they were putting in. No one had seemed enthusiastic about even doing this, and now he was hiding in a corner of a room, surrounded by people who wanted to torture and interrogate him, with no assurances that the plan would even work.

Looking up at the monitors, though, he remembered why he had done all this: in a corner of one screen, two boxes displayed images of the real Puck and Irene, stripped and standing in rooms the size of coffins.

He was doing this for them. Seeing them like that and knowing what they must have been through reminded him that he wanted to be here, to help them.

Meagan, the operator communicated neurally to—Moss assumed—the cadet. *Can you check on the camera in G1?*

Ugh, I'm on break, she answered, confirming Moss's suspicions. *Can I check it in a few?*

No, the operator told her. *There's a little surprise waiting for you in there.*

If it's garbage, I'm gonna come back there and kick your ass, Meagan threatened. Moss watched the feed from the break room as she stood, lurching to her feet unenthusiastically.

Moss shook with nerves as he realized she would miss the stolen key card as soon as she got to the garage. He wanted to spit. How had he not anticipated this?

Weary and disappointed in himself, he pulled his Kingfisher and waited.

He watched the security feed as she walked down the hallway and got to the door and his heart nearly burst from his chest as she felt around her belt. She shrugged and shook her head before turning back, and Moss watched as she headed back down the hallway.

Moss pointed his weapon at the door as he heard a light knock.

The operator grumbled and pressed a few buttons on his keyboard. The door opened dangerously close to Moss and the cadet stuck her head in, blond wisps falling in front of her face from a loose bun as she made an exaggerated grumpy expression.

"Lost my card," she whispered.

The operator swiveled in his chair, nearly kicking Moss. His cloaked weapon was pointed directly at the cadet as the operator said, "Again?"

"Fuck off," Meagan said. "It's only the second time! Can you run it back, and we'll see where I dropped it?"

The operator snorted. "Like I told you the last time and will no doubt tell you again the next, I can't replay videos without logging the reason. So, unless you want to explain to my superiors that you lost your card like a dope, I can't help you."

Moss had never been so grateful for red tape. He and his friends had spent countless hours bemoaning the tracking and logging ThutoCo did but now, it was finally helping him.

"Fine, I'll retrace my steps then, but it means I can't check that cam now," the cadet said.

The operator smirked. "Too bad."

Meagan huffed. "Why, what was the big surprise?"

The operator chuckled. "Oh, yeah, just Alex and Anthony from R and D having sex in the garage."

Meagan's eyes went wide. "No shit? Don't they know they're being filmed?"

"Maybe they get off on that?" he suggested.

Meagan tilted her head and pointed at the obvious erection

in the man's pants. "Don't think they're the only ones getting off."

"Get the fuck out of here before I report that you lost your card again," he said, sounding genuinely hostile.

She stuck her tongue out at him and shut the door.

Moss felt like he could puddle onto the ground. His nerves were frayed, and he just wanted to get this over with and get out.

Now was the time.

He closed his eyes and tried to focus but was too distracted by everything that had just happened.

He curled up, pulling his knees against his chest, and tried to clear his mind.

Thoughts continued to pop in, one after another, and while he felt as though he was flashing into the program, when he tried to connect, it flittered away.

He thought about the last time he had been able to get there.

He was stressed and scared, and it almost seemed to be driven by his own mental overload.

He focused on the fear in the moment, curled up surrounded by enemies, but that didn't work either.

He gritted his teeth, hating himself for not being able to do it.

Then he opened his eyes. He looked up to the bank of monitors, to Irene's naked form in the tiny cell. He thought about her touch. The false her in that bed and the real her here being prodded and invaded so they could get to him.

The anger rose within him as he stared at her in the upright metal coffin.

The corners of his vision began to blur as he reached out with his mind for the program.

Just then, her head moved, and she looked up at the camera and into Moss's eyes.

. . .

MOSS SMILED as he looked around his hex.

It had worked. He was equal parts thrilled and terrified as he now had no idea what his physical body was doing.

He hurried over to his desk within the program and sat, wondering how he could access his father's presence in the future. He looked at the simple menu laid out before him on the screen. It showed a green bar filling quickly.

LOCAL SYNCHRONIZATION COMPLETE

He grinned. His mind had begun the process without consciously thinking it.

He found DRUDGE MANUAL OVERRIDE and clicked through.

A voice emanated from the terminal. "Would you like to take manual control of the local GERTA model drudge?"

"Yes," he said and hoped his body didn't mutter.

His vision quickly became that of the camera display from within a drudge.

UPLOADING displayed in the corner above the HUD.

He wondered what was uploading as he looked around the room, trying to figure out where the drudge was.

UPLOAD COMPLETE

"Moss?" He heard a robotic voice so familiar it sent shivers down his spine.

"Two?" Moss gasped. It had been so long since he had heard his robot counterpart's voice, it felt like a lifetime ago. ThutoCo would have combed through every moment of interaction between Moss and his AI partner after he had betrayed the company.

"You've been a naughty boy," MOSS II admonished.

The familiarity was replaced with terror. "Two, is this personality flagged?"

"I'm afraid I can't answer that," Two told him. Moss had been happy for just a moment to be reunited with Two, but he now understood that it was a trap. ThutoCo technicians had left Two's program in the system to synch with Moss in case he ever tried exactly what he was doing in this moment. He had played right into their hand.

"Shit!" Moss said, trying to think of what to do.

"Use of such language is unadvised, and you will be docked one Productivity Point for the day," Two informed him.

"Override security," Moss shrieked.

Two didn't answer for a moment. "Please provide override password."

Moss had no idea what to say or do. No display showed and he felt hopeless. If ThutoCo was informed that the MOSS II personality been activated, they would get a fix on his location instantly and all of this would be for nothing.

"Override accepted," Two said.

Moss gasped, "Thank you, Mom." In that moment, he understood just how powerful a program his mind contained.

"With that out of the way, how have you been, Moss?" Two asked casually.

He couldn't help but chuckle at the question. "Fine," he said. "A lot's changed."

"I'm sure," Two said. "You swear more now."

Moss outright laughed at that. "Right. You'll be happy to know I also have robotic legs now."

"Oh, welcome to the club," Two joked, and Moss smiled for a moment before realizing just how strange it was that one of his oldest friends was a machine with a personality based upon his own.

"Where are we?" he asked, getting to business.

"We are in ThutoCo Facility 39-67 on the continent of Africa," Two said.

Moss groaned; it was taking him a moment to remember

how to get answers from his drudge. "Where, specifically, is this drudge in the facility?"

"Ah, this facility-maintenance GERTA model is on a recharge pad on floor three. Battery life is at forty-six percent," Two said.

"Right, that should do for now," Moss said. "Let's go to prisoner holding."

"As you have security clearance, prisoner holding is an acceptable designation," Two informed him as the machine stepped from the pad, out the door, and to a wide corridor. "I assume you wish to avoid contact and would prefer the stairs to the elevator?"

Moss was happy that Two was programmed to acknowledge his desires. "Yes."

An indicator appeared, marking the location of the destination as the machine moved toward the staircase and descended. Moss asked, "Does this drudge have any weapons?"

"This unit is devoid of weaponry," Two said before adding, "but it has hands."

Moss understood what Two was implying. He knew he didn't need to make small talk with an automated personality, but he couldn't help himself. "Any news from the home front?"

Two let out a digital laugh which always made Moss cringe. "Much, but relevant to you would be that Ira was promoted in the absence of Mr. Greene."

"Oh," Moss whined. "Fuck that guy. I assumed management was smarter than that."

"Options were limited after," and Two paused for effect, "certain actions were taken, and many employees left the company."

Moss smiled, happy that what he had done really did have an impact, however small. He was also pleased that overriding the security measures seemed to stop Two from noting Moss's language.

"How has the mood been at the company?" Moss asked. He had been removed for so long that he was genuinely curious about how things were going back where he had grown up.

"You caused quite a stir and you're on everyone's lips, even if they don't know your name," Two told him. "People were very upset at the implication of malfeasance, though the company did much damage control. I'm now programmed to inform management of dissenting opinions. People have said ThutoCo now feels more like Carcer Corp."

Moss laughed. "Trust me, it's still nothing like Carcer," he said, before amending, "except in their unified goal of oppressing the people of this planet."

"That is something I am programmed to report," Two said.

Moss paused to think a moment. "Two, if you have not been used since my last log in, how do you know these things?"

"My AI learning is updated regularly and includes company-wide information," the machine told him. "Even while being stored on the servers, I am updated regularly."

"Fascinating," Moss said.

The screen flashed that they were approaching the holding cells. "Can you bring up a feed from within the room?"

"Certainly," Two said and an image of a BurbSec officer eating a sandwich in front of the doors to the holding cells appeared in the corner.

"And while we are at it, add another one of the control room," Moss said, and another box entered the screen. He knew his body was in the room, though he could not see it. "Let me take manual control."

He felt the movements of the drudge as his own. He held a metal palm with digital imprint up to the keypad and the door opened. He stepped in quickly, and the officer only had time to look up from his sandwich, eyes wide, before a steel fist came crashing down on his head.

"I took the liberty of looping the feed before entering the room," Two offered helpfully, and Moss watched in the corner of his vision as the guard sat, chewing the same bite ad infinitum.

Moss hurried over to the row of holding cell doors and said, "Good thinking."

"However suspicious," Two added.

"Right," Moss chuckled as he held a palm to one of the locks.

It beeped in recognition of proximity but flashed red. "This unit is not approved to open cells," Two explained, though Moss had already reached that conclusion.

He felt for the keycard from the cadet before realizing it was back with his real body and moved the drudge to snatch the one off the felled officer. He opened one of the cell doors, and Irene looked at him with confusion; part of her head was shaved and stitched crudely.

"What's all this, then?" she asked, and Moss felt a strange twinge as he heard her real voice for the first time. Though it was the same, it felt different to hear.

He cleared his throat, the sound odd through the little speaker and said, "My name is Moss. I'm with Detritus Sixteen out of BA City, and I'm here to free you."

Her long eyelashes fluttered as she blinked with confusion and her face turned hard.

"This a trick or a dream?" she asked dubiously.

Moss had the drudge gesture to the guard on the floor. "Neither," he said. "We have little time and are surrounded by enemies on all sides. I'll free your brother and we'll get out of here."

"Don't suppose you brought any clothes?" she asked as he moved to the other cell and opened it.

"Sorry," he told her, and she stepped out on shaky legs and grabbed the officer's weapon.

The second door opened, and Puck looked at the machine before him. "What?" was all he said.

Moss was cut off before he had a chance to speak.

TRANSMISSION INCOMING.

A familiar face filled his vision. He had never met the man, but Moss knew him instantly.

"Employee Moss, it's a pleasure to finally speak with you. I'm Arthur Smith, President of ThutoCo," he said.

"Shiiiit."

CHAPTER 15

"You were clever to try and shut down the information flow, but unfortunately computers relay information more quickly than humans," Arthur told him. "I presume you are still in Africa, and we are working to find your location now so we may send some friends to greet you. Shouldn't take long. Your mother was good, but my people are better."

Terror filled Moss as the man spoke. He was one of the most powerful humans on the planet with an army of Zetas at his disposal. Moss had known what he was doing was risky and the threat of capture was omnipresent, but this made it more real. Moss watched as Irene spoke to Puck though the partially translucent image of Arthur Smith and wondered why the man had revealed that he didn't know where Moss was.

Mute transmission, Moss commanded Two, and the face in his vision became another small box on the screen.

"We have to get out of here!" he said aloud to Puck and Irene.

She had Puck's arm slung over her shoulder. He seemed in much worse shape than she was in. "Surely we will arouse no suspicion such as we are," Irene said. Their bruised, naked forms glowed in the bright fluorescence. He felt bad for not thinking to bring them clothes, but he couldn't dwell on it.

They had to go.

Loop all feeds, Moss told Two, continuing to use the neural commands.

"Can't mute me for long," Arthur said. "I told you my men are good."

"The fuck do you want?" Moss asked him as he told Two, *Get me to my body.*

The drudge began moving with Irene all but carrying Puck a bit before Moss turned the machine and picked up the nearly limp body.

"Cheers," Irene said and raised her weapon as she followed the machine.

"I simply wish to speak with you, Moss," Arthur said.

Moss could see that the man kept looking away from the camera, no doubt receiving information and giving neural orders. He was clean-shaven and wearing a crocodile smile. His face betrayed his age, the skin pulled tight from too many injections designed to maintain a youthful appearance. Though his eyes were bright, dark purple streaks lay just below the skin. He obviously didn't sleep enough.

Moss laughed. "Just want to speak, huh? You send a lot of guns after a person you just want to talk to."

"Figured you might take some persuading, and anyway, they are all set to stun," Arthur said in a tone so convivial as to be off-putting.

There was no one in the hallway, and they had not yet alerted anyone to their presence, and Moss couldn't help but wonder what Arthur actually wanted. The man was smart and calculating and must have some goal in speaking to him, even if Moss didn't know what.

"Why did you try to kill everyone?" Moss asked, hoping to throw the man off.

He chuckled lightly as though he had been asked something entirely benign. "You have a very confused idea about me, Moss. Why don't you just come back home, and we can talk about it."

He hated that Arthur kept using his name.

Moss heard the crack of Irene's pistol and watched in his main field of vision as a BurbSec officer dropped as he rounded a corner.

"See you soon," Arthur winked, and the box went black.

"Shit!" Moss screamed. "Two, take control and bring them to my body in the control room."

"Certainly, and. . ." Two said.

"Yes?" Moss asked before returning to the program.

"Goodbye," Two said, sounding sad.

"Hopefully I'll see you in just a moment, but I take your meaning," Moss said. "Nevertheless, goodbye, Two. Hope to work together again sometime."

HE WAS BACK in his hex.

He needed to exit the program. He had spent so much time trying to figure out how to get in that he had completely ignored thinking of how to get out. He stood up from his desk and paced around the room.

"This is all in my head," he reminded himself.

He tried thinking of Irene and Puck, using the thought of them mostly defenseless to try and extract himself.

It didn't work.

"Fine," he said and rushed back to the computer.

Bringing up a feed, he said, "Grandma, ThutoCo knows we are here. Set up defensive positions at the garage, and I'll try to get to you when I can."

"If they're wise to us, they'll be sending an army. Get out quick," she answered.

"I fucking know it!" he yelled and cut the transmission.

He turned and screamed to the ether, "Get me out of here."

In some vague way, some way he couldn't understand, he felt a toe twitch.

"Yes, sir," he heard through the speaker in his hex, and he knew that the operator had received orders.

He felt trapped, stuck behind a barrier in his own mind.

Closing his eyes, he focused on the toe.

He remembered his friends in peril and tried to move his body in the real world.

He felt another twitch, beginning to feel confident as he wondered what was happening in the world around his body.

He focused now on his eyes, his mind, and his consciousness.

He tugged, pulling with psychic energy.

He saw white close in.

Blinking, he stood, back in his body.

His legs carried him easily up as his hand moved, his mind in a daze. He didn't feel himself pull the trigger or the recoil of his weapon as he fired at the operator's nape. He moved as if floating to grab the weapon off the man's hip. The screens upon the desk displayed lines of code. The operator had no doubt been working to regain control of the cameras.

Moving to the door, he looked around and saw Irene hustling behind Two toward the door. Puck's head rolled this way and that in the robot's arms.

"This way," Moss said, pointing.

"An apparition!" Puck wailed in confusion.

Moss had forgotten that he was cloaked but chose not to appear. "I'm invisible but here," he told Irene.

"Your bag of tricks is deep," Irene said, looking vaguely in his direction. "My brother is in a bad way."

"I know, we will get him help when we are clear of this," he assured her. "Two, we are going to the garage."

"ThutoCo Zetas are inbound on this position," Two informed him, and Moss felt odd speaking to him separately. They had always been joined, and now MOSS II was as an independent entity, controlling the drudge on its own.

They moved to the door, Moss and Irene pressing their bodies on either side.

"Ready?" he whispered and she nodded. Two fell in besides Moss as he opened the door and entered the garage. The light clicked on, but they saw nothing. Moss activated the control, and the door began to open as they all ducked behind the garbage cans.

Moss saw Sandra, Anders, and Ynna in defensive positions behind a van as the door opened.

He had just enough time to think they had made it before the Zetas had arrived.

The van began to crack and clank as they descended on their position. The three began to return fire as they quickly retreated into the garage.

The street grew dark as the sheer number of Zetas blotted out the sun. As they landed, they moved in and formed a semi-circle around the mouth of the garage. One of them was pointing and barking orders and getting answers that filled Moss's mind. The commander's chest erupted with blood from a shot from behind, and all the Zetas turned to return fire.

"Now," Sandra screamed, and they all began to fire at the Zetas as well. More landed in confusion and sent so many bullets into the garage that the walls began to explode out at them and made them feel as if they were being shot at from all directions.

Two turned to Moss. "Take him," he said, handing over Puck, who slumped into Moss's arms.

"Not really the time," Moss hollered over the racket.

"I'm. . ." Two began and stopped speaking as the Zetas cease their fire. The world felt silent and ominous.

"We have you surrounded," Arthur Smith's voice said coolly from the drudge's speaker.

"I know that voice," Sandra said from the other side of the garage and raised her weapon in the direction of the machine.

"No need for that and no need to die here," Arthur told them. "Let us return our employee to the safety of his burb, and you can all walk out of here free."

"You ain't got a brain in your nut if you think I buy a word of what you're selling," Sandra said.

"You would rather watch your grandson die here?" he threatened.

Sandra didn't even pause. "Yes."

"Sad," Arthur said and Moss, for once, agreed with him. They were surrounded, outnumbered, and trapped.

"You're also a fool to think me one," Sandra said and sprayed the drudge with a burst of bullets. Hot metal showered down on Moss, who turned to protect Puck's naked form from the shrapnel.

Sandra's voice rang out in Moss's head, *Now's the time*, and he had no idea to whom she was speaking.

Tires screeched outside the door and the Zetas all turned.

Moss watched in elation as they began firing to the side and a massive beast came careening toward the throng, impaling a Zeta as it was riddled with bullets.

More came behind it, and the street became a confused mass of Zetas and Bovidae Biotechnics's genetically modified monsters. Blood sprayed, muzzles flashed, and smoke filled the air. Sandra charged forth with Ynna and Anders right behind.

Moss heaved Puck up, and Irene stopped him, grabbing at an invisible form.

"Thank you," she said, somehow managing to meet his eyes. "For coming for us."

He thought of all the reasons he had done it. All the guilt he had felt and said, "You're welcome."

She snatched the second weapon from Moss's hand and moved to enter the fray.

He yelled to her, "Stay behind me."

She couldn't be stopped and burst forward, firing with both weapons into anyone and everyone. She looked full of rage as she shot at her tormentors.

Moss lay down covering fire and moved to try and help her, but he couldn't simply leave Puck, unsure if they would have time to go back and retrieve him.

"Irene," Puck croaked helplessly as he watched his sister, reaching out to her with an unsteady hand.

A beast picked up one of the Zetas and tore them in half, showering the street in crimson.

Moss watched in horror as the naked form of the woman kept striking forward, firing shot after shot. Even amidst the cacophony, a few Zetas took note of her and turned to fire.

Anders and Ynna shot the Zetas dead, and Sandra shouted, "Get into cover."

Irene took no notice of the words. Puck was limp, his body an obvious representation of the damage that ThutoCo had done. Irene had seemed normal to Moss, and he hadn't stopped to think of the mental toll their experiences had taken.

Ynna rushed from cover and speared Irene in the ribs to get her to safety.

It was too late. One of the Zetas shot her through the exposed chest, and blood sprayed Ynna who wailed, "Shit," as they crashed to the ground.

Another of the beasts—this one covered in ornate tattoos between slow-release vials sown into its flesh—tore the Zeta's arm from her body and began beating her with it. She screamed until she was silenced, and Moss dragged Puck toward his sister.

Ynna sprang up. "The fuck was that?" she asked as she turned to shoot at a few of the remaining Zetas who were beginning to flee.

Sandra and Anders moved out to keep them covered as Puck looked at the form of his sister, tears in his eyes.

He turned to Moss. "Give her peace. Let her not see all this."

Moss bit the finger of his glove and pulled it free from his body. A single floating hand exposed. He reached down and closed her eyes, touching her flesh for the first time.

The Zetas had fled, and the hulking people were snorting and looking at one another. Seeing no more of their enemies, they stretched and cracked knuckles as they moved out of sight toward their vehicles.

"We have to go," Sandra said as Anders moved toward Moss to help Puck to the car.

Moss scooped Irene into his arms.

The torment she had experienced so that ThutoCo could find Moss had driven her over the edge. He felt guilt and hate in a way he had never known as he carried her limp body forward. Puck was weeping softly, and Moss vowed that he would see Arthur Smith and the company pay for all this.

He would get whatever technology Carcer was to unveil this week and use it to bring them all down.

As he lay her down in the truck, he whispered, "I'm sorry."

CHAPTER 16

The mood was low.

Everyone seemed lost in their own thoughts as they stood over the grave. Irene was laid to rest next to her family. Puck, who was recovering slowly, stood staring at the unmarked plot next to his sister. His plot.

He turned to Moss, still angry and miserable. "When all is said and done, I appreciate you coming for us. We were not long for this world. They spoke of doing us in, and you saved one life though you lost the other."

Moss knew the truth in his words. ThutoCo was likely waiting on approval to murder the siblings. It didn't make him feel better. He blamed himself for everything that had befallen the two.

"What will you do now?" Moss asked him.

Puck looked far away. "I owe you a debt of gratitude and will help you in whatever way I can, after which time I will retire from this life. It was Irene who wished to act as heroes, and I see now the cost.

"The people of this city will have to soldier on with one fewer advocate, such as I was."

Moss nodded slowly. "I understand. If you wish to return with us to BA City when we are done here, you are welcome."

Puck gave a weak smile. "Appreciated, though I think not. Through no fault of your own, you will always be inextricably associated with the death of my sister, and I don't wish to lay that burden upon you."

"I will bear it regardless," Moss told him honestly.

Puck's face contorted in miserable understanding. "It's an odd thing, mortality. All the advances, all the technology which separates us from our predecessors, and death unites us. We fly from it. We fight it. It matters not. It catches us all."

Moss thought of Rosetta, Burn, Chicken Thumbs, Stan, and Irene. All the friends he had made and lost. His parents, taken from him and erased from his memory. He looked at his grandmother, standing with his best friend and his new ones.

Death was coming for them all.

He thought then of Arthur Smith and Alice Carcer, two of the planet's most powerful people with armies at their fingertips. Both searching, hunting for them.

Moss wanted to spit, to scream. More than anything, he wanted to stop them, to keep them from doing to others what they had done to him.

Puck turned to Moss, resolve mixed with profound sadness. "How may I be of service?"

"Let's find out," Moss told him, and they walked over to his friends and family.

Sandra was explaining to the three, "I fed them misinformation that ThutoCo was making a move against them. Bovidae intercepted what they thought was an encrypted internal memo. Got Seti to scramble communications so I could give them orders to attack the Zetas. Few things better than getting one company to do your dirty work against another."

"No wonder you were a successful general," Gibbs said, astonished.

Sandra grimaced. "We're outnumbered and pursued, so we have to be smart. Always."

"We won't be outnumbered forever," Moss put in. "One day, we'll wake the world."

He received nods all around, except by Puck, who was lost in thoughts once more.

"What happens now?" Ynna asked. She seemed more herself, and the tension between her and Gibbs appeared to be resolved after their talk.

Moss was happy for that. He knew they needed to be a unified front if they were going to pull off this next job and get out of Africa alive.

"Now," Sandra told them. "We go to a party."

The casual way she said it elicited chuckles from the group.

"How?" Ynna asked.

Sandra shrugged. "I'm having Seti investigate ways of infiltrating the building. Security will be higher than anything we've ever faced so it'll be an uphill battle from the jump."

"Why not simply walk in the front door?" Puck asked with a hint of his bravado returning.

"We'd be shot to death," Sandra put plainly.

Puck smiled slightly and shifted uncomfortably in the sweatpants and tee-shirt featuring a cartoon dog they had provided him. "*You* would be."

"What are you rambling about?" Sandra asked impatiently.

"Masks," he said. "The classic ruse is classic for a reason."

"That's what I always suggest!" Gibbs enthused.

Sandra snorted. "I hate to tell you, but a pair of glasses and fake mustache won't fool even the dolts who work for Carcer."

Puck chuckled. "Moss has told you of my aversion to technology no doubt, but that doesn't mean I don't know a good idea nor that I am unfamiliar with modern advances."

"You're talking about genetically engineered skin masks?" Anders asked and the rest of them caught up. "You must know one hell of a biohacker."

Puck crossed one foot behind the other and gave a sweeping bow. "That I do."

Sandra held up a hand. "Even if you got us these masks, they wouldn't let just let us waltz in there."

"Certainly," Puck agreed, "but if you took the place of some invited guests, you could copy their genetic material for look, fingerprints, and even gen tests if it came to it."

"Masks," Moss found himself laughing.

"Masks," Puck smirked. "How many of you were you hoping to smuggle in?"

Sandra looked around at them. "Anders will need to be ready with the ship, and Gibbs can keep eyes from nearby, so, just the three of us. Unless you're keen to join us?"

Puck shook his head. "Oh, my, no."

"Just three then," Sandra told him.

He stroked his chin and stared at them for a long while. "I know just the people."

"We don't have much time," Sandra reminded him.

"Then away we shall," he said and took one last look at his sister's grave.

THEY HAD ABANDONED THE VAN, so they hurried after Puck on foot. The cold and wet of the previous day had been replaced with the brutal sun to which Moss was still not accustomed. The heat made the manure-laden air thick and oppressive. The graveyard was in a part of the city which Puck had explained was among the poorest, and people littered the street, taking shelter in the shade of tall tin buildings that looked more like houses of cards than proper homes. Workers were everywhere on the buildings, soldering pieces into place while holding cheap goggles to their faces for protection.

"Anywhere else, drudges would be doing this work," Gibbs pointed out.

Puck agreed. "Quite right, *anywhere else.*"

He held up a hand to a cabbie, waving him over and negotiating a fare in some local dialect. He slid the door to his cab open with cracked and calloused hands. The air inside was stagnant and hot, dust from the seat cushions billowed into the space as they piled in.

"Where are we going?" Gibbs asked as Puck joined the driver in the front of the ancient car.

He looked back at them. "Pumayyaton's Tailor shop."

"Fuck," Sandra said. "We ain't got time to go for a shop."

Puck guffawed. "Oh, but we must. We can't call on the wealthy dressed as vagabonds. Nor, I presume, do you wish to attend the gala dressed thusly."

"You know who he reminds me of?" Gibbs whispered under his breath.

Ynna nodded as Moss said, "I already told him."

The car shook violently as it sputtered to life, and they began a long drive, which consisted of the driver screaming and swearing at anyone unlucky enough to share the road with him. They zoomed through the streets, bouncing and skidding the whole time.

"I miss automated drivers," Gibbs announced, clutching the windowsill and looking as though he might vomit.

The slums seemed to stretch on interminably before they pulled onto a freeway, the city passing like a blur.

They stumbled out of the car, looking worse than after a firefight, when they arrived at their destination. Only Anders strode out easily, his body accustomed to the rigors of space travel.

Puck paid and thanked the man and turned toward the building with mannequins draped in fine suits and gowns in the display window.

Bleary-eyed, Sandra turned to Anders and Gibbs. "Don't need you for this bit. Go have a drink."

There was no love lost between the two, and Moss wondered why she would send them away together before realizing that was the point. Sandra was smart and trying to ensure all internal conflict was resolved before they ran a mission in which they would all need to have one another's backs.

Seeing the wisdom in her action, Moss could not help but think of Mr. Greene, his old boss from ThutoCo, who loved to wax at length about corporate policy and leadership in management. "A good leader hires capable people and gets out of their way. The more you tighten your grasp, the lower the output becomes. A real leader listens first and speaks second. You provide your people with what they need when you can and explain yourself why you can't when that's the case.

"When conflict arises, you model the behavior you wish to see and help without intruding."

The words rang true as he thought about his grandmother. She had a firm hand, there was no doubt, but she let Ynna do what she needed to when the time was right and encouraged dialogue without forcing the issue. In that moment, he began to truly understand how she had led people into war.

Gibbs scowled but Anders smiled. "No arguments from me."

He clapped Gibbs on the back, causing him to wince, and they turned to find someplace to have a drink. If Moss knew anything about the world outside the burbs, it was that there was *always* a bar nearby.

"Puck, my friend," a balding, middle-aged man said as they

entered the shop. He wore a tight black dress and tall, heeled shoes encrusted with jewels. He had bright, brown eyes, light brown skin, and ornate cybernetics that covered half his face. They were of gold etched with black and had a ruby-colored eye in the center.

Puck moved to embrace him, asking, "Curtis, how are you?"

"Better than the bedraggled man before me, I think," he said, appraising Puck. "Pea is pregnant again, and we welcome our first son any day now."

"That makes five, congratulations. Send her my undying love," Puck told him.

He smiled. "For us, as with all species, children are the meaning of life, yes?"

"Quite," Puck said, sounding a little uncomfortable.

Curtis looked over his shoulder to the three of them.

"You brought friends, but not Irene. Where is your beautiful sister?" he asked.

Pucks eyes welled instantly, and Curtis moved to hug him again. "I am so sorry, old boy."

Puck had seemed to be rebounding quickly, but Moss knew the truth of it: he would never get over this loss.

Moss admitted to himself that he wouldn't either. He would do what he always did and try to focus on the next goal and remind himself that what he did was for the greater good. He would, though, in the quiet moments, think of her and the others they had lost.

Ynna shifted uncomfortably as Puck wept, and Curtis looked over his friend's shoulder and told them, "Why don't you begin looking around?"

They nodded graciously and did so.

Moss made his way over to racks of tuxedos. The place was dimly lit with maroon carpets and fine chestnut walls lined with tall mirrors. The clothes looked complicated, and he searched for the clip-on bow ties he had seen in movies, but to no avail.

Ynna walked over with several dresses slung over one forearm. "I can help with that stuff," she offered.

"Thanks," Moss said, genuinely grateful.

Ynna smiled. "No problem. My dad used to make me help him tie his ties when he was too drunk to do it himself."

"Right," Moss said. "I sometimes forget you came from money."

"Wait 'til you see me in this dress. You'll understand what designer babies are all about," she quipped, but there was a note of sadness in her voice.

"He still alive, your father?" Moss asked.

Ynna dropped her head. "Don't know, don't care. The last time I heard from him, he told me not to tarnish the family reputation. Pretty sure that ship has sailed."

A silence descended on them. "You doing okay?" she asked to fill the void.

"Not really," Moss admitted. "It's sometimes too ugly and brutal a life."

"It's an ugly and brutal world," Ynna said, before adding, "but you're doing well though, despite it all."

"Thank you," Moss said. "You and Gibbs okay?"

He surprised himself by asking the question, but he was so tired and overwhelmed that he didn't feel the need to play coy.

Her face indicated that she was surprised as well, but she nodded. "Yeah, for now. We talked. He's just such a delicate fucking flower that it's hard most of the time. Bad things happen to the people around me, so I struggle..."

She trailed off.

"I can relate," Moss said.

She smiled and said, "I know," before turning to a rack and

pulling off a black tux. "Here, try this," she held it out, and they both moved to spacious changing rooms.

As he dressed, Moss couldn't help but marvel at how soft all the items were to the touch. Having spent his young life in coarse linens, hardened by too many industrial cleanings, followed by secondhand items bought from street vendors, the fine slacks were like nothing he had ever experienced. He was impressed that Ynna had picked something which fit him so well without spending much time even really looking.

He tucked the shirt in, pulled the vest on, and finally the jacket. He felt as though he was being choked as he buttoned the top button at his neck. Turning to see himself in the mirror, he did a double-take. In a world of selfies, he spent almost no time looking at himself, but he smiled as he turned and posed.

He unearthed his Kingfisher from the bundle of clothes on the bench and held it up with both hands, feeling like a debonair secret agent.

He put his gun away and exited the room.

"Well, hello Mister Bond," he heard Ynna say as he stepped into the showroom.

"Right?" he said, thrilled with the reaction.

He turned and his eyes went wide. While he was not intellectually attracted to her, Ynna was undeniably beautiful. She cocked an eyebrow as she caught his look and held her arms out before giving a little spin.

The red dress was so tight that nothing could be worn underneath, and it hugged her form as she moved. Slit down the front to her navel and backless to just above her rear, she looked good and knew it.

"Wow, Ynna," he sputtered.

She winked. "Yeah, pretty sure that's what he was going for when my father designed me."

It was an odd concept to Moss: the idea that a parent would be so concerned with the looks of their daughter above all else. "You resent it?" he asked as she watched herself move in a mirror. She pursed her lips slightly at the question and turned to face him again.

"I don't even know anymore. I didn't, then I did, and now I just try to accept it as part of me," she said and ran a finger along her wrist where the skin met her cybernetic hand.

"I guess we are all trying to do the best we can with the hands we were dealt," Moss said, checking to make sure his grandmother wasn't within earshot.

"That's just it, isn't it?" Ynna asked. "We can't help what came before, just what we do."

Moss nodded.

Ynna ran her hands down her body to smooth out the fabric. "Comes in handy sometimes, anyway."

"Don't you two look dapper," Sandra said as she came out from a changing room wearing a wide, dark blue gown with white ruffle accents. "Now all you need is a corsage and boutonniere."

Ynna rolled her eyes. Moss shifted awkwardly as he thought about the prom held in the burb and the girl he had asked when he had really wanted to take Issy.

"I got so fucked up before our school formal that I hardly remember it," Ynna told them and appraised Moss. "You did not."

He shrugged. "I did not."

Puck strode over confidently, tapping a new cane as he walked. He had on a cheerful smile, but his eyes were puffy and red. He wore a green checkered suit with brown leather gloves and boots. An umber top hat had his signature gold gear affixed to the black hatband.

Moss wondered if Curtis had a whole stockpile of clothes just for him.

"These clothes come as my gift to you as I will expect you to pay Synthanee yourselves," he announced.

They all thanked him, and he waved them off with false indifference.

"Can we get this show on the road?" Sandra asked, pulling uncomfortably at a thread in her gown, causing Puck to wince.

"We shall," he said and gestured to the door. He looked at Moss as the women moved to exit.

His eyes were miserable as he pointed to Moss's suit and said, "Irene would have liked this. You are just her type."

Moss shuddered. He had never known her, but he would avenge her.

CHAPTER 17

Sandra decided to give Gibbs and Anders more time to talk, so the four of them walked down the streets in their finery, turning heads wherever they went. Being sniffed by strays, stepping over garbage, and ignoring pleas for money was made all the more difficult by their attire.

They approached what looked like the door to a bank vault with cameras on either side and mounted guns beneath.

"Nope, it's not obvious at all that shady shit goes down here," Ynna mocked.

"Please refrain from that tone when we enter," Puck scolded. "Synthanee is not a woman to be taken lightly."

Ynna scoffed. "Whatever."

Puck waved a greeting to one of the cameras and the door groaned, moving backward before rolling aside. He gestured and they stepped forward into a steel-plated anteroom. Brightly lit and unadorned, the room felt like a cage as the door closed behind them. Information gathered from biometric scans appeared on a screen projected onto one wall.

"Master Puck," a voice called out through a speaker. The voice was low and measured and thickly accented.

Puck looked to one of the cameras mounted in a corner and spoke. "My new friends and I have rather a large job we need done quickly."

"That, you know I can accommodate, but can I trust your *new friends*?" the voice asked cautiously.

"On my life," he said, voice cracking.

"Then your friends will be mine, but trust is a fickle mistress," she said and one of the steel plates swung open.

Moss could not believe his eyes as they entered the warehouse-sized room of computers, lab tables, and eerie, low, green-lit vats. The large tubes had submerged printers quickly fabricating sleeves of skin while others housed full, anatomically correct suits of skin slit along the back. Eyeless faces stared at them from racks of jars along the walls. The overwhelming smell of chemicals filled their noses, and Moss had a hard time not pinching his nostrils.

They all took in the scene in astonishment. Moss had heard whispers of this kind of work but had never thought he would see it firsthand. It was dangerous and the companies were rumored to shut down the operations whenever they were discovered.

A woman in a lab coat stepped around from behind a bank of monitors. Her head was shaved bald, and her large cybernetic eyes reflected an unnatural emerald color in the light of the room. Her naturally dark skin was made light with an obvious lack of exposure to the sun.

"Synthanee, it has been too long," Puck said with a sweeping bow.

The flat look on her face did not change with the greeting. "Formalities bore me. You know this."

"My apologies," Puck said. "It has been a bit of a hard time."

"It is a hard time for all of us, always, Master Puck," she

intoned. "Furthermore, I did not think you approved of my work, as so many do not."

"While I certainly prefer rubber and glue, these are desperate times," he explained.

Her head cocked nearly imperceptibly. "Do not speak to me of desperation, speak to me of need and payment."

"You're a blunt woman and I can appreciate that," Sandra interjected, Synthanee's eyes moving slightly to gaze upon her. "We fix to infiltrate that Carcer gala and need false faces to do it."

"That party is this very evening, have you the genetic material I require?" she asked.

Puck stammered, "Not yet but I know who they mean to impersonate so you can begin the fabrication."

"I presume you also need my supplies to acquire what I need for this job?" she asked.

"We do," Puck said.

"I do not like to rush, and my work already does not come cheap," she told them, her voice remaining tempered.

"We can pay," Sandra said.

"And we come to you because you are the best," Puck added.

Synthanee blinked slowly. "I am the best precisely because I do not rush, and flattery does not interest me."

Sandra huffed. "Can you do this job or not?"

Synthanee made a clicking sound with her tongue. "You have an odd way of ingratiating yourself to potential business associates."

"Sorry," Sandra said. "We're on a clock here, is all."

"Understood," Synthanee said. "You and I will work out finances as you appear to be the leader here and I will take some samples."

"What kind of samples?" Sandra asked, and for the first time in his life, Moss heard fear in his grandmother's voice.

"For the skin to move naturally and appear as real, the inside must fuse to your own," she said as though it did not need to be explained. Moss saw the light glint off a single bead of sweat on Sandra's brow.

"Alright," she said.

"It will be more difficult to cover that hand," Synthanee told Ynna, pointing slightly before turning. Ynna flexed her metal fingers.

Seeing his grandmother's reaction and seeing the vats of skins, Moss was more than a little unnerved. His cybernetic legs and the program in his mind were already leaving him with questions and now, the idea of wearing skin modeled after another person and fusing to his own, put him ill at ease.

He looked at Ynna, who seemed to be having the same reservations. She was shifting uneasily, her eyes darting around the room.

They were made more uncomfortable when a drudge, with a torso of skin pulled tight over its chassis, emerged from the darkness.

"Hey, Puck, how's it hanging?" the drudge asked in a high-pitched, friendly tone.

"Greetings, Vince," Puck said with a grimace.

The drudge cocked its robotic head. "You gonna tell me again how you hate the way I was programmed to talk?"

"Probably," Puck said with a slight nod.

Moss was shocked by the way the drudge spoke. The eastern American accent felt completely incongruous with both the woman he had just met and the surroundings.

The drudge turned its faceplate to look at them, two red dots serving as eyes.

"Synth programmed my personality based on a friend of hers that died, you got a problem with that?" it asked.

"No," Moss said.

"Definitely," Ynna said, seemingly without thinking.

"Honesty, I like that," the machine said, pointing to Ynna. "Yous two follow me and we'll getcha sampled."

The drudge turned and they followed. Puck caught Moss's eye as he began to walk. "Through the looking glass now," Puck said more ominously than he likely intended.

As they navigated between the vats, Moss couldn't help but think of his father's work. Copying personalities was a technology that was supposed to only be used to make working with the drudges easier for the operator. Hearing Vince speak, Moss realized the other potential application of keeping a loved one's spirit alive after their death. It was, of course, not the actual person, but perhaps it could help to bring solace to some.

Synthanee seemed to be alone in the world but was clearly comforted by having even a programmed version of her friend around. With the programmed version of his father, Moss felt the same way, and he wondered that if things were different—or if ThutoCo was a different kind of company—if perhaps the technology could be used for good? He didn't have the time to ask himself if this use would be good though as Vince gestured for the two of them to sit.

"Lose the jacket and roll up a sleeve," it told Moss.

He did as instructed, and the machine pulled a medical device off of a metal tray. The clink sent a chill down Moss's spine. Though it felt like a lifetime since he had awakened in the Carcer holding facility, it had only been a short while and the memory was still fresh. The drudge curled its metal fingers around the device and pressed it against Moss's skin.

"Taking a skin sample," Vince told him. "I'm told it doesn't hurt but what the fuck do I know about it?"

Ynna scoffed. "Pretty self-aware."

Vince let out a synthesized chuckle. "I think therefore I am and all that."

"Deep," Ynna joked.

"I like your hand," the drudge chided back and pulled the trigger. Moss hardly felt it, but he still winced.

The drudge moved the device and screwed it into a large computer tower for analysis.

"You watch how I did that?" it asked, turning red dots on Moss.

He nodded. "Pretty simple."

The drudge made a sound akin to a flatline. "You say that now," it said in a way that made Moss nervous.

It sampled Ynna quickly and walked them back to Puck, who was standing before a computer monitor with an image of a wealthy family posing in front of a large, ornate staircase.

"These them?" Vince asked.

Puck said, "Yes," as Moss got a closer look at the family. There was an older woman standing with her two adult children, wearing fine clothes that looked not too dissimilar to what they were wearing now. The young man was of a slightly fuller build than Moss, and the young woman was shorter than Ynna, but they would certainly pass. The older woman was much younger than Sandra and wore a broad smile that Moss had never seen cross his grandmother's lips.

"Their estate is close to here, and it will be the work of but a moment to get what we desire," Puck informed them.

"We are just going to walk right in?" Ynna asked dubiously.

"Quite," Puck said, tipping his hat.

"You've got a brass pair, I'll give you that," Vince said, cupping one hand.

"I sincerely. . ." Puck began but fell silent as Sandra and Synthanee returned.

Sandra looked pale and Moss wondered what Carcer had done to her for all the years in captivity.

"That's gonna be me?" she asked, pointing to the screen.

Ynna shot her a smirk. "You even remember how to smile?"

Sandra didn't take the bait. "Guess it'll be nice to recapture my younger days."

"Skin is but a façade, not a fountain of youth," Synthanee said.

Sandra sighed. Turning to Puck, she said, "Your friend and I have made arrangements. Let's go steal some identities."

CHAPTER 18

Standing before the door of the estate, there was an undeniable sense of nervousness in the air. Puck had brought the sampling kit in his satchel, and Synthanee had begun work on the masks, using collated images for the design and their genetic materials for the innards.

The plan was a good one but the three of them were uneasy and Sandra's clear distaste was as a gray cloud over the whole affair.

Puck was ignoring their misgivings and strode forward to a gate set into a tall marble brick wall topped with imposing metal bars hooking outward toward the street. Guard drones circled overhead as men and women in uniforms tended the garden between the wall and the home itself. In the heat of mid-morning, the groundskeepers' sweat showed through their shirts, lining their backs and underarms.

The house was tiered and cubic, with glass windows and fencing on the balconies. Designed to look modern, Moss couldn't help but think that it looked like the architect let their child stack blocks and designed a home modeled on that.

The size of it was impressive. The grounds alone seemed as

large as a city block, and the house itself seemed to stretch and jut endlessly. In BA City, affluence manifested differently. The height of one's apartment and the number of floors one owned were a sign of wealth. Moss wondered if it was different here because the tallest towers were filled with cows and stank, so the wealthy wanted to show their status horizontally rather than vertically.

Puck stepped forward to a camera bulb. "Greetings, ASH, is the mistress of the house in?"

A voice piped from a small speaker answered, "Is she expecting you?"

"Oh, my, no, I come with belated birthday wishes and bearing gifts," Puck told the automated system.

"Standby," the system said.

Moss sweltered in his layers as they waited.

"ASH," Ynna said with a hint of a smile. "Think this house has a boomstick?"

Grinning, she looked to them expectantly. Puck and Sandra looked to Moss who didn't get the reference either.

Ynna huffed and folded her arms. "The *only* time I need Gibbs, he's not around."

"Sorry," Moss said as though he should have understood.

Ynna rolled her eyes. "At least he watched old movies. What did you do all the time in the burbs?"

Moss shifted, wishing the house would let them in. He thought about all those nights in his hex, plugging his mind in to watch his favorite reality competition shows from the audience.

"Nothing," he finally admitted.

"That's what—" Ynna began but the intercom cut her off.

"The mistress of the house will see you now," ASH informed them, and the thick glass door slid into the wall, allowing them passage.

Moss tried to calm his nerves, taking deep breaths as they walked through the garden. The drones hovered over them as they walked along the recently swept brick path. A small pond full of large fish burbled on one side of them, and an old man used the tiniest shears Moss had ever seen to groom a bonsai garden on the other. Small replicas of fantastical homes were set in among the plants, and Moss couldn't help but gawk at the diorama. The little village circled around an active fire pit no bigger than Moss's fist and a path lead up toward a larger building with a steepled roof.

"The way some people spend money," Sandra scoffed, and Puck cleared his throat to silence her.

They approached large mahogany doors with knobs of gilded gold. A woman in a tuxedo even finer than Moss's opened the door for them and another waited inside. She gestured with a white-gloved hand for them to follow her. They walked past a pristine open room which was empty except for a man seated at a piano with an accompanying violinist standing beside. The house read their temperatures and blasted them with individualized air conditioning as they moved. Speakers carried the music being played in the other room with them as they continued down the hallway hung with family portraits. Unlike the image from Synthanee's lab, no one smiled in the pictures. They wore severe, standoffish expressions.

For such a large home, it felt more lifeless and sterile than even the burb had.

They were guided into a large sitting room in which all the chairs faced a fireplace taller than Moss with a holoprojected fire dancing within. A table was set with small sandwiches, thinly sliced meat next to a slight bowl with sauce dotted with seeds, peeled cucumber slices, coronation chicken on a bed of romaine, and scones plated next to a silver hot water pot.

As Moss stared at the food in wonderment, Ynna chuckled.

He remembered that she came from money and had likely seen spreads like this her whole life.

"Do they just leave this out all the time?" he asked her.

She opened her mouth to speak but Puck introjected, "Can you play at being patrician for even a moment?"

They fell as silent as scolded children, but Moss made his way over to the table. The food looked wonderful and he figured he had to try some of it if it was just sitting there.

Ynna clicked her tongue and he turned to see her shaking her head.

He wanted to ask what the point of all this food was if not to be eaten, but he didn't, instead moving to sit in one of the large chairs.

Ynna shook her head again. He let out an exasperated sigh and stood still, his hands clasped behind his back. At this, she nodded.

Puck was pulling small artifacts and trinkets from his bag and setting them on a cloth he had unfurled on the table with clawed legs. The furniture was both elegant and modern, as if someone had taken the designs from Puck's home and redesigned them with computers.

All heads turned as Klasina Van Dijk entered the room followed by a white dog that looked to Moss like a cotton ball with a face. She wore an elegant maroon gown and beamed when she saw Puck, taking no note of the other three.

"My dear," she said as she gave Puck a delicate hug, her hands draping for just a moment on his shoulders before she pulled away. "Come bearing gifts, I see," she announced, looking to the table.

"In more ways than one," Puck told her, pointing a flat hand at the three. "May I present, Sandra, Ynna and Cesario, new associates of mine who are helping me to expand my business."

"Delighted," she said without looking at them.

Moss couldn't help but notice that he was the only one among them who warranted a false name, and he wondered how many people in the world knew of him.

"It's wonderful that you are expanding, my boy," she said to Puck as she sashayed toward the items on the table. "If it means you will be bringing more items such as these."

She plucked a muted blue faience scarab off the table, running her hand over the smooth surface.

"Are the children about?" Puck inquired, sounding less casual than Moss imagined he had hoped.

Klasina did not take her eyes from the item in her hand. "They will be joining us presently. With such a glut of wardrobe offerings it takes them an age to dress on the best of days."

"You will be attending the gala this evening?" Puck asked.

"Oh, my, yes," she said and flipped the scarab to examine the underside. "You know, Alice Carcer is a close personal friend."

Moss saw his grandmother's face twitch, and he readied himself should she bolt to pummel the woman.

In that moment, the absurdity of his own life struck Moss. He had come so far and seen so much to be standing in this fine home, so different from any world he had known. He had all the amenities in the burbs, but they had been given to him to keep him complacent, keep him working without asking questions. This home was like something out of a fever dream of opulence, and yet he stood poised, waiting to stop his grandmother from attacking someone.

He wanted to laugh.

He did not.

"Any word on what might be unveiled this evening?" Puck asked her as she set down the scarab and moved on to a jewelry box.

"I wouldn't tell you even if I did," she said absently.

Puck laid a hand on his chest. "You wound me."

She looked up at him sardonically, her voice low. "We tolerate you because of what you do for us, but don't think for a moment that we approve of your extracurriculars."

Puck's face fell flat, and he did not speak. After a moment, she returned to examining the treasures.

Moss didn't know what to do with himself. It was awkward to stand there and watch the moment play out while feeling like little more than statuary.

The white fluff of a dog cocked its head as the children entered the room. Puck had explained to them that Aya and Sander were the type of rich elite that people loved to hate, as images of their most recent trips around the world often flooded their palmscreens.

Sander wore a powder blue tuxedo with ruffled shirt and Aya a red dress similar to that of Ynna. Sander made his way directly over to Puck and swung his arm with an aggressive handshake. They made small talk as Aya made straight for Ynna.

"I don't know you. You're pretty," she complimented with a hint of derision.

Ynna affected a vapid voice. "Right back at you, girl."

Aya cocked her head and smiled as if she was happy to meet someone who could play the game. "So, what, you know Puck?"

"Through work," Ynna offered.

"Lame," Aya stated.

Ynna smirked. "We all can't just hang out on yachts all day."

Aya screwed up her face. "Ew, jealous much?"

"I also brought a treat for us to enjoy and a very special item," Puck announced to the room.

Aya shot Ynna an icy glance that Ynna fired right back.

"What's that?" Sander asked.

Puck pulled a box from his bag. "Tea," he told them, and no one looked impressed.

"I prefer something stronger," Sander said. Moss watched

the way he spoke and moved in hopes of trying to emulate it later.

"This tea is made from a plant long extinct on this planet, and I assure you, you'll forget all other drinks when it touches your lips," Puck explained theatrically, making his way over to the table to begin filling cups with hot water.

"And the special item?" Klasina asked, sounding intrigued.

Puck said over his shoulder, "For that, I must insist that the help be sent from the room."

"Are they even in here?" Klasina said, looking about and waving the men and women in the corners and doorways away.

Puck dropped teabags into the steaming water and began to distribute the cups. Moss examined the fine China, looking at the delicate, exquisite artwork along its face. He took a sip, knowing his was not laced.

When Puck had explained the plan, Moss had asked what made the tea so special. Puck had laughed and said, "Affluence placebo, my boy. There is nothing remarkable about the tea except the yarn I weave. Being told it is lovely will make it so, to them. I do not know if thinking it is rare actually makes it taste better to them or if they simply ignore the taste because they have been told it is wonderful.

"Either way, the con is always a success. With the wealthy, you must understand, it is the label more than the contents."

Moss had raised an eyebrow at the assertion, but now, seeing Aya and Sander sip and make contented sounds, he realized the truth of it.

Klasina did not take the drink; she simply held the cup in her hand and watched her children.

Moss became worried and felt his hand move toward his belt.

"None for you?" Puck asked coolly. Moss could see the

tension on his face though. Their whole plan was predicated on them going down without a fight.

Klasina gave no hint of what she was thinking. "Not just yet. I very much would like to see what is so special that you needed us alone."

Aya wobbled and put a hand on Ynna's shoulder. Her head rolled and her face flushed as she told Ynna, "I don't think I like you."

Ynna removed her hand, sending her tumbling to the floor. "Feeling's mutual."

Klasina opened her mouth to scream, but the instincts that Moss had and still didn't fully understand were quicker.

The Kingfisher was loose in a flash and he fired a bolt that dropped her instantly. Puck moved to catch the unconscious woman as she fell.

"The fuck?" Sander asked, eyes red and confused. He was looking at them but not seeing or understanding. The drugs coursing through him had taken effect though not entirely. His hips swayed and a leg buckled before he, too, was on the ground.

Sandra shot a scathing look at Puck. "Damned fool," she snarled. "They may be down, but we are surrounded on all sides. Those stuffed shirts sure as shit will call for help the moment they see this mess."

"My dear," Puck said, carrying Klasina's limp body toward a painting of yellow hay bales in a field. "You know nothing of the rich."

He lifted a boot and quickly kicked the painting from the wall, saying, "Sorry," to—Moss presumed—the artist. A digital keypad with fingerprint reader was exposed as the painting clattered to the floor. Puck lifted the woman's hand in his own, pressing her thumb against the reader.

They heard a quiet click and Puck moved along the wall and

pressed his boot against a vent at the base. A piece of the wall swung open to reveal a spiral staircase.

Ynna chuckled. "My house had a couple of these."

"If you wouldn't mind," Puck said, gesturing for Moss and Ynna to pick up the children and follow him up the stairs. "Servants are not allowed in the living area when the family is at home. We will be safe."

"What about ASH? Will the automated home security pick up on this?" Moss asked.

"Oh my, if you believe this is the first time any of them have been carried to their rooms in a stupor, you're fooling yourself."

Moss shook his head as he grunted to lift Sander. A human body was heavy and awkward, and his grandmother helped to lift the legs. Ynna slung Aya over her shoulder with relative ease. A soft piano concerto followed them up the stairs as they ascended.

At the top, Puck guided them down a white carpeted hallway to one door.

"How do you know this place so well?" Ynna asked and Moss had been wondering the same thing.

"Sander's taste runs to the more... discreet," he said suggestively, opening the double doors into a room with a bed larger than the safe house they had been using.

They lay the unconscious bodies on the floor, and Puck took the samples quickly. Moss was struck by how seamlessly this plan had gone. Puck had come up with easy and elegant solutions to everything, and it had run just the way he had envisioned.

So many of the plans that Moss had been a part of had gone belly up very quickly, and he thought that he should try to learn from Puck. Perhaps he could give them more insight and help with the forthcoming part as well.

He roped, gagged, and placed the three in bed for good

measure as Ynna made jokes about how much the man carried in the shoulder bag.

As they moved to the roof, where a large black car sat on a charging pad, Puck turned and spoke. "Some light auto theft and our business will be concluded. Any of you drive?"

Ynna didn't speak and simply opened a door and moved into the driver's seat. "Not really driving," she huffed as she turned on the computers and cleared their departure with the security drones. Puck slid open a passenger door that gaped into a massive backseat like that of a limousine. Long leather seats flanked a bar with chilling champagne.

They clambered in and Puck wasted no time in extracting the bottle from the ice and popping it open. He called Syntha-nee's address to Ynna so she could program it in and began pouring glasses as the car lifted slowly and began its glide.

"To new friends," he toasted, and Moss looked at him quizzically.

"What will you do now?" he asked.

Puck looked far away for a moment and then took a slow sip. "I don't know," he said finally. "I'm not even sure how present I am now. I feel like a light in a deep fog. Losing Irene was always something I knew to be possible yet it felt distant. Without her, I'll be lost."

"I'm so sorry," Moss found himself saying again.

Puck shrugged. "And after this," he continued, waving a hand around the car. "My life will be forfeit anyway."

"What?" Moss asked, but Sandra nodded grimly.

Puck looked him right in the eyes, his face sullen. "You heard the woman. I have been allowed to operate because I grease the right palms and give the right people things which they want. Now that I have betrayed the elite, I have given up what little cover I had."

Puck dropped his head.

"Come with us," Moss said, less as a suggestion and more of an order.

"No, my place and fate are here," Puck said without looking up, his eyes simply following the cascade of bubbles in his glass.

Moss wanted to scream, to slap the man. Looking at him now, he felt the same grim helplessness he had with Irene in her final moments. By taking them to the house and doing what he had, Puck was inviting the same fate as had befallen his sister.

"No," Moss said, putting down his glass.

Puck's eyes did not move as Moss produced his Kingfisher again and fired a single shot.

"What the fuck?" Ynna screamed, looking back at him.

"Moss!" Sandra called simultaneously.

Shock registered on his grandmother's face as Moss put the weapon away slowly. "Tell Anders to put him on the ship."

Sandra looked at a loss for words. Shaking her head, she said, "It was his decision."

Moss looked right at her with serious surety. "It was the wrong decision. By his own admission, his mind was clouded by loss. I won't allow him to die, not like this, not for this."

Sandra's eyes told him that she understood.

"Now, let's go steal some tech and get the fuck out of this city," he said, grim determination in every word.

PART III

CHAPTER 19

After making their preparations at the lab, they were now ready to attend the gala. Moss looked at himself in the reflection of the car's window as it flew over the city toward the spotlights in the distance. He smiled and frowned as another man's face made the actions back at him. It was one of the strangest sensations he had ever experienced.

He hardly felt the synthetic skin upon his own, but when he wrinkled his nose, it was Sander's nose that wrinkled back at him. His eyes though, those were his. He turned them on Ynna and his grandmother who looked equally lost in thought.

The little white dog sat in Sandra's lap. Moss had not even noticed it follow them up the staircase and into the car, and they decided to take it with them despite Sandra's protestations. She scratched its head absently as the car began to descend.

It was an odd thing: going straight into the belly of the beast without sneaking and skulking.

Gibbs was finding a place to keep an eye out, and Anders was sitting with the ship. Seti, the real Seti, was on comms and everything was ready. This moment would define them.

Surrounded by Carcer on all sides, they would either leave with the stolen technology or die trying.

Moss had been in situations like this before. He felt as though these were the only situations in which he found himself anymore. Still, it made him nervous and tense.

The car moved into position behind several others and idled. They looked out the window to see a line of beautiful vehicles in a line, moving toward a red carpet surrounded by press.

The dregs for whom they fought would be spending their evening watching as the wealthy poured into the convention center to celebrate Alice Carcer and learn of her new advancements. It was strange to think that so many of the poor still worshiped the rich, believing the false claims that it could be them someday.

The car glided forward smoothly, and they watched as an obese older man, sweating in his garish attire, hauled himself out of a car to wave at the cameras. He was quickly followed by a beautiful woman, easily twenty years his junior, who strut and posed as if she were at the end of a catwalk.

"Some things never change," Ynna groused.

Sandra scoffed. "And all I got was this fucking dog."

"Gotta love being a woman," Ynna joked.

Moss knew better than to add anything to the conversation. They pulled forward and a man opened the door for them. As they emerged from the vehicle, bulbs popped as flashes filled their vision like an electric storm. Media members called their names, pleading for them to stop, pose, and answer questions about who they were dating and about their latest escapades. Ynna took to it naturally and Sandra played along, shooting a smile so unnatural as to be a grimace. Moss gave a little wave, palms damp and heart thundering. He could hardly see and wondered if it had been a mistake to impersonate such high-profile individuals.

The small dog, that Puck had told them was named Lord something-or-other that Moss could not remember but who Ynna just called Perro, stopped on the red carpet and turned to face the various cameras. Moss couldn't help but be amused that the small animal, raised by the wealthy, was much more comfortable in the situation than he was.

They moved toward the entrance, pretending that they were far too important to answer the cries of the media. Large digital posters of Alice Carcer loomed over them from either side of the entrance, her stern face with piercing blue eyes staring down at them. One of the screens fizzled a moment and displayed the words, "Corporate logo," above, "Corporate catchphrase" before returning to the image of the blonde woman.

Moss wondered if some lackey's head would roll for the momentary lapse.

They ascended a wide staircase to a security checkpoint. Large men made even larger by bulletproof vests worn under their tuxedoes, blocked the doorway.

"Hand," one of them told Moss in a gruff, heavy tone.

Moss presented his hand and the massive man pressed an electronic device no larger than a pen against his fingertip. Moss tried to breathe slowly, but the air caught as he felt the prick. He felt his heart pounding but attempted to act cool.

The machine flashed red.

The second man lumbered a step closer.

The first held up a hand to stop him. "Fucking machine. Sorry, Mister Van Dijk, we will need to try again."

"No problem," Moss said meekly. The respect the man was showing him would evaporate instantly if they realized he was not who he said he was. These guards were threading a delicate needle: they needed to be reverent of the guests, but only to a point. Their presence was an inherent threat, but they could not be discourteous.

The man pulled Moss's forefinger and he stopped breathing altogether.

"That better not be a drug test," Ynna joked playfully, waving her small purse at the guard.

He looked up at her, stone-faced. "It isn't," but then he smiled just for a moment and winked.

The pen flashed green and he waved Moss through. He felt as though he might collapse, and that was just getting in the door. Despite everything he had been through, he didn't know if he was up for the task. Seeing Irene charge those guards had made him question his foresight and situational understanding. He had thought himself smart but continued to find himself in situations that left him questioning that. Burn had been smart, his grandmother was, and Puck had proven how clever he was, but Moss doubted himself.

He had gotten far on instinct but would need much more than that if he was going to be successful. Ynna, too, had shown how talented she was. Joking with the guard and easing a tense moment, she was smart and capable.

He waited just beyond the guards and was joined a moment later by his grandmother and Ynna. They began to walk toward the din of the party down a wide hallway. Vidpic images lined the walls, showing man's history with space travel. Moving images of rudimentary spacecraft, grainy videos of scientists and control rooms, and the early Deyus ships blasting off before finally, pictures of the colonies.

"Moss, you've got to calm the fuck down," Ynna said under her breath, putting a hand on his back which startled him back to reality.

Sandra hissed, "None of that. From here on, we are our faces."

"Sander, you got to calm the fuck down," Ynna corrected.

"I know. I'm trying," Moss said, his words sounding pathetic even to himself.

"Just remember who you are," Ynna told him and gave his butt a little pat. It was meant to be endearing, but he was so concerned with playing the part, nothing could calm him down.

The little dog padded along, holding its head high as they stepped into the ballroom. There was a stage with a podium at the front and a screen at the rear that looked out over a dance floor populated by people talking and eating the finger foods circulated by waiters. The dance floor was surrounded by tall tables without chairs, and there were four bars where drudges were making drinks with robotic efficiency. Teardrop-shaped lightbulbs were suspended from the ceiling on wires and oscillated between red, blue, and white lights.

A choir stood to one side, singing a halting choral theme where low baritones pounded as high sopranos pierced in intervals, meeting in a grim motet. The music gave the room a vaguely militaristic feel, which was no doubt what Alice Carcer was going for. The Carcer guards who lined the walls of the room were dressed as military officers throughout history: Akkadian archers, Spartan spearmen, centurions, Vikings, Huns, medieval knights, western cavalry, World War-era infantry, and modern corporate shock troopers were all united by the red scorpion pincer logo of Carcer Corp emblazoned on their helmets.

Moss found himself feeling more surrounded by the enemy than he had in Carcer City.

"Klasina!" a woman called out and waved Sandra over to a small group.

She gave the false smile she had been practicing and made her way over, saying, "Hello, my dear."

"And then there were two," Ynna said ominously.

The moment didn't last as Moss caught the eye of another

young man, who gave a head nod and beckoned for him to join them. Ynna waved him away and said, "You got this, Sander." She emphasized his name for effect, and he puffed himself up, trying to play the part.

He approached the group of men, all clean-shaven Caucasians in their twenties.

"Hey, Sand," the man who had called him over greeted. "Whiskey rocks?"

Moss nodded and the man snapped at one of the others who hurried off to get the drink. Moss didn't know what to say. He felt lost among these people with whom he was supposed to fit in.

He thought back to his days in the burb when Gibbs would invite him out to watch the Miners matches with some of his work friends. Moss always felt out of place then too, drinking his beer quietly as they tried to impress one another with knowledge of sports and tales of their latest conquests. He tried to think back to how they spoke, trying to recall attitude and phrases. Mostly hoping for those nights to end, he had never imagined his life would depend on a recollection of them.

"What's up?" was all he could muster, but it seemed to do the trick. The men were all drunk and smiled at the question.

"Just got back from Osaka this morning," the lead boy said with a broad smile. "You know me, nose to the grindstone... and by grindstone, I mean sake bombs!"

They all laughed and high fived, and Moss smiled along. "Aya is looking fiiiine," he said, putting a heavy hand on Moss's shoulder.

"That's my sister!" Moss said instinctually.

The kid laughed it off. "You telling me you wouldn't hop that grade A?"

"No, man, I wouldn't fuck my sister," Moss said, grateful as the other boy returned with his drink. He took a quick gulp, the cool liquid burning right into his bloodstream as the ice clinked against his face.

"I would," the boy said, squeezing his shoulder.

Moss turned a clever face on him, feeling the drink instantly. "Fuck your sister? I bet you would!"

The other boys all laughed and cheered the comment.

"Oh, shit, Benedict, he got you!" one of them cried.

Benedict's face fell. "Not cool, man, Bella is in the hospital."

"Oh, shit," Moss said seriously. "Sorry."

Benedict burst out a laugh and said, "Nah, I'm just fucking with you. She's fine and fiiiine."

All the boys laughed along, and all Moss could think of was Ynna saying, "Gross."

"You about ready to turn this party up?" Benedict asked.

Moss had guessed this would become an issue. He did not want to dull his wits or be out of control of himself for what was coming, but he also didn't want to blow his cover by acting out of character.

"You know it," he said, hoping he could figure a way to pocket a pill or fake an injection.

"Yeah, I do!" Benedict announced and clapped him on the back, the whole herd of them trooping out of a side door and toward a bathroom. The hallway was bright after the shifting dim of the ballroom, and Moss took a second to adjust his eyes with Benedict pushing at his back.

They burst into the spacious restroom, which had a small lounge area at the front and a bank of sinks across from the stalls.

"Good evening, sirs," an attendant greeted them as they entered, some of the boys falling into lounge chairs and spilling their drinks.

Benedict approached the man, his tired face watching the

drunken youth. "You know who I am?" Benedict asked assertively.

The man nodded, his graying beard bobbing slowly. "Yes, sir."

"Then you'll know I'm being straight up when I tell you it'd be best for you to wait outside. Getting you fired wouldn't be the half of it. You'll be sucking dick for figs if you don't scram. Get me?"

The man lowered his head. "Yes, sir," he said with such dejection that Moss wanted to put Benedict through the wall then and there.

He didn't. He played along and pretended to laugh with the rest of them. He would have his revenge when they used the Carcer tech to bring down all the assholes like Benedict.

It was why he was here, why he was in a bathroom wearing the face of another man.

Their goals often felt distant, but as the man shuffled out of the room, Moss remembered who he was fighting for.

Benedict pulled some baggies of pills from his jacket pocket and laid them on the faux marble countertop. "Got some morning sunrises, event horizons, hazy fogs, and dark nights," he offered all around.

Moss didn't know what the various names meant, but he was relieved that they were pills. He could get away with not taking them one way or another.

"Morning sunrise," he said, figuring that would be something which would likely speed him up rather than slow him down if some seeped onto his tongue before he could spit it out.

"Knew you would want to hit the ground running," Benedict grinned, pouring some pills out and producing a heavy plastic card. Gathering the pills slowly, he placed the card on top and began grinding them down to a fine powder.

Moss reeled, trying to think of a way that he could pretend to take the drugs. He couldn't come up with a way out. He began to work on a distraction, something to take their attention, but he was too slow. Benedict cut out some powder lines and pulled a small length of metal tube which he presented to Moss.

"Age before beauty," he smirked.

Moss took the metal in an unsteady hand. He had no idea what effect this would have and how it would affect the rest of his night, but he had no other options. He considered just saying no but reminded himself that they needed to fit in a while longer.

He put the tube to his nose, pressed a finger against his other nostril and inhaled deeply.

CHAPTER 20

The effect was instant.

His heart hammered, his fingers tingled, and he looked up at the mirror over the counter in time to watch his own pupils in another man's face dilate. He felt a rush as though he was being flung down an elevator shaft and he gripped the lip of a sink.

"Do it!" he heard in a familiar voice, sounding like it was calling to him from the far side of a tunnel. He saw flashes of his hex and knew the program was firing.

"Do it! You know you want to!" the voice called again.

He couldn't pinpoint it.

Trying to blink didn't help. He felt trapped between the real world and the one in his mind.

He saw his father shaking his head disapprovingly.

He saw Issy, concern written all over her face.

"That's why you are there, right? End her and be done with it!" He knew the voice. It was on the tip of his mind, just out of reach.

"Shit, I want in on that," a voice from near his ear. The real world.

"Yeah, man, ride that shit." Benedict's voice.

Moss saw Sander's face staring at him. Then Sander collapsing back at the estate. Images moved and distorted before being replaced.

Moss tried to focus on his breathing, on his mind, on anything he could hold on to.

He saw his own face staring back at him. Digital distortion, like a computer monitor on the fritz. His face jerked and stuttered. Arthur Smith's face stared at him with a gruesome smile.

"Kill her and be done with it!" he cried.

That was the voice.

Was it a hallucination? A message?

Moss opened a dry mouth somewhere, trying to speak.

Silence.

No bathroom, no hex, just white.

"Good stuff, right?" Benedict asked and patted him on the back before squeezing the nape of his neck.

Moss saw the room, the kids, himself. He let out a long, labored breath.

"What?" he asked to no one in particular. Still feeling the effects, he wanted to ask a million questions, rush out, and tell his grandmother what he saw.

He did not.

"Let me know if you want more," Benedict offered and bent to snort.

Moss moved around on shaky legs and turned on the sink, scooping handfuls of water into his mouth, sending much of it cascading down his shirt. He ran his wet hands over his face—feeling no water, just the touch—and through his hair, trying to figure out what he had just experienced.

"I'm good for now," he mumbled to Benedict, but the man's mind was elsewhere.

Who did Arthur Smith want him to kill and why? If it was just his mind playing tricks, who did *he* want to kill and why?

"I feel like we should go back. To the party, I mean. We should be there. Don't want to miss anything. I mean, I don't know what there is to miss but I don't want to, you know?" he heard the words pouring from his lips as Benedict seemed to refocus on the moment.

"You know what I was just thinking?" Benedict began, all the boys wrapped in drug-induced laser focus, listening intensely as they made their way back to the ballroom. "The characters in *Any Given Match Day* are a perfect allegory for where the actors were in their careers. You know? Hear me out."

He continued to speak as they all walked in. He went on and on as Moss looked for Ynna and his grandmother.

"What you think, Sand?" Benedict asked, sounding as though he sincerely wanted affirmation of his idea.

"You used allegory wrong," Moss said absently, scanning the crowd and realizing the false faces made picking them out more difficult.

Benedict snorted. "Asshole."

"No, sorry, it's a good point," Moss told him the same way he did with Gibbs when he would make similar points about movies Moss had neither seen nor cared to analyze.

"Ugh," Benedict groaned. "I really don't want to have to listen to my aunt give another speech. These things are so boring and repetitive."

Moss's mind reeled at the new information. His "friend" was Alice Carcer's nephew. That had to be good news for them. He tried to figure out ways he could use that to accomplish his goals. The notion of finding Ynna evaporated quickly. He needed to stay by Benedict's side.

He came up with a plan as Benedict continued, "Blah, blah

we are the world's greatest private military. Blah blah, we have some new toy."

"Blah blah, world domination," Moss piled on and Benedict guffawed.

"Exactly! So fucking one-note," he chuckled.

Moss came up with a plan, his eyes scanning the room. The drugs had made him feel more focused than he ever had in his life, and he acted as a machine targeting his prey.

He found it in a statuesque blond. She was tall and beautiful with a curvaceous figure hidden under a tight yet modest gown. With little exposed skin, she was exactly what Moss was looking for.

"Oh, man," Moss said, letting his eyes guide the other boys. "I'd kill to see what is under that dress."

Benedict followed his gaze. "You and me both, brother. Molly Compson never shows off the goods, though. Dare me to run over there and pull a tit out?"

Benedict started to move, nearly salivating at the idea of it. Moss put a hand on his chest to stop him.

"I've got a better idea," Moss said, letting a wicked smile cross Sanders's face. Benedict was all ears.

"After the speech, what say we use that family name of yours to get into the control room and play with the cams. Bet you anything they got some x-ray shit we can use," Moss offered, not knowing if it was true.

Benedict's eyes went wide. He gripped Moss's chin and looked him right in the eyes. Moss worried if the false skin would shift to the hard touch, but it did not. "That's where it's at!" Benedict said. "Now I can't wait to get through this speech."

Moss let his face grin stupidly as he was released. "I should go check in with Mom before I get too schnockered," he said. "I'll find you right after the speech."

"I know you will," Benedict said with a wink and turned to the others.

Moss made his way quickly through the crowd. The changing lighting made picking people out difficult. He spotted Ynna at a bar, faking a smile to a young man looming over her. Moss strode over and announced, "She's out of your league."

The bearded man with hair coiffed just-so turned drunkenly to Moss. "*No one* is out of my league."

"My sister is," Moss said and the man grimaced.

He turned his eyes back to Ynna and winked with the subtlety of a car crash. "I'll find you later."

"Oh, great!" Ynna said, her sarcasm lost on the man. "What's up?"

"Gotta find my. . ." and he hesitated, remembering to play the part. "Mom."

They moved together, both working to try and find Sandra. She was in a circle of older women chatting loudly and laughing theatrically.

"Oh, Mother," Ynna said, extending a hand to tap Sandra on the shoulder.

She turned with a flourish. "Oh, hello, dear," she said, nearly spilling the drink as she moved. Moss knew that this half-drunk glass of champagne was not enough to get his grandmother even tipsy and that she was putting on a show for the ladies.

"Can't I get five minutes peace from you children?" Sandra asked with pronounced condescension.

The women laughed. "This generation can't go five minutes without suckling at the teat," one woman said.

Another added, "I'm sure they need money."

They were all giggling as Sandra informed them that she would return and pulled the two aside.

"I'm trying to get a read on these women and gather intel. What could be so important?" she asked harshly.

"I wouldn't have pulled you aside if it wasn't important," Moss hissed. "Things are going to happen fast after the speech, and since they clearly have a dampener blocking neural transmissions, I needed to tell you now."

"What's up?" Ynna inquired.

"One of Sanders's friends is Alice Carcer's nephew, and I got him keen on breaking into the control room with me after the speech. If you guys can get a fix on where the package is going, I should be able to deactivate the dampener *and* open doors for you so you can steal the tech and grab Alice," Moss explained.

"Lucky break," Ynna said, rolling her eyes. "As always, with you."

Moss snorted. "I doubt it. I'm pretty sure Puck picked these people precisely because of these types of connections."

"Kid's smart, I'll grant you that," Sandra said. "You make that all happen, let us know and make sure Anders fires up the ship. I ain't losing anyone this go-round."

"No problem," Moss said, pleased that things seemed to be working out, though the sense made him nervous. Plans had seemed to be working out in the past before going sideways very quickly.

"I've been flirting with guards and should be able to lift some weapons without them noticing," Ynna put in.

Moss scanned her over. "Not sure you would be able to hide a weapon."

Ynna scoffed and unslung the purse from her shoulder. "Boys are so stupid. Betcha didn't even notice the purse."

Moss had to admit to himself that he hadn't. The drugs had given him a sense of hyper-awareness, but he had missed the purse entirely.

"Enough of this, we have parts to play, so let's get to it," Sandra said and turned to walk away.

Ynna was still shaking her head at Moss. "You think you can do this? I can come with you, work the computers if you need?"

"No," Moss told her. "Got him going up to perv on one of the girls here, and I think if he sees your tits, he'll forget all about the control room."

Ynna's eyebrows raised, a familiar expression even hidden under Aya's face. "Tits, eh? What are you, high?"

"Yes," Moss said simply.

Ynna groaned. "Well, that's fucking great."

"Playing a part, remember?" he said. "Anyway, I got to get back to it."

"Just keep your head in the game," Ynna called after him.

"Always," Moss called back over his shoulder; the words lost amidst the din of the party.

Moss sidled up to Benedict who turned, looking disappointed. "Thought you might've brought your sister over here."

"Nah," Moss said, shaking his head and gesturing. "Let's focus on Molly. That's a piece we can both enjoy."

Benedict nodded his agreement and Moss was happy and a little dismayed that the drugs seemed to be unlocking some inner asshole. Benedict continued to talk about work, and Moss half-listened until the lights all at once changed to a dim white, the stage became illuminated, and the choir concluded the song.

All eyes turned to the stage.

A spotlight from the back of the room sent a bright beam to the curtains off to the right. Alice Carcer stepped forward, striding confidently toward the podium. She wore molded black armor over a black bodysuit with the Carcer logo prominently displayed upon her chest and shoulders. Though wiry thin, she looked fierce, like a starved dog ready to pounce on the first thing that crossed her path. Her blond hair was pulled tight against her scalp into a braided ponytail without a single strand out of place.

A long, curved sword hung from her belt and swayed as she marched forward. Even from afar, she was intimidating. Not just the power she wielded but the woman herself. Moss felt a shiver run down his spine just being in her presence.

For the first time since walking in, fear truly gripped Moss. He worried that they had walked right into a trap. Perhaps she would point a slender finger at him the moment she turned, and he would be shot dead where he stood. His body trembled as her piercing blue eyes faced the crowd.

They began to clap politely before erupting into thunderous applause, everyone in the audience seeming to try and outcompete their neighbor for adoration.

"Here we go, blah blah," Benedict joked.

Moss hissed for him to shush.

"Alright, shit, sorry," Benedict whispered. "Never took you for a sycophant."

"Greetings, one and all," Alice Carcer began and the cheering quieted. Her voice boomed through the speakers and was much lower than Moss had imagined from such a diminutive person, sounding more like an older man than that of a woman. He wondered if she had voice modification software installed but stopped thinking as she continued. "Welcome to the eighty-second annual Carcer gala. As some of you may know, though this company is now hundreds of years old, this party began in a rented barn as a way to celebrate the founding of the Carcer Corporation. Those early attendees were happy just to be out of their fatigues for one night," she joked, and there was a smattering of laughter. Though she had walked out as though she commanded the room, Moss thought he noticed a sense of nervousness as she spoke.

"This gala has become an unrivaled event since those humble beginnings, and I am thrilled to be sharing this evening with you all. Without the people in this room, what we have accomplished so far and what we strive to achieve in the years to come would not be possible. Thank you for being here."

More applause followed. "When the pandemic first struck this planet, the Carcer Corporation was a humble company whose only goal was to aid nations in need." Benedict snorted a laugh. "When the world began to face a war with the infected, and governments began to collapse, this small group grew into a military force which would go on to save the planet from a self-inflicted extinction event."

The audience roared once more.

"She knows how to fire up a crowd," Benedict noted under his breath.

"We have now expanded to become the greatest private military the world has ever known. Our officers keep more than two-thirds of this planet's citizens safe. This past year, with the completion of the Ice Block facility where those with only the highest bounties will find themselves, we have a presence on every continent. We are truly a global force the likes of which the world has never seen, nor ever will again."

More cheering and, with the drugs coursing through him, Moss's patience was wearing thin. He wanted her to reveal whatever it was she was going to and exit the stage so they could get on with their plan. His fears of a trap were not assuaged but became less intense as she continued to speak. "As we have now secured this planet, it is time to take our business beyond our current borders."

A hush fell over the room as a burly man strode onto the stage, a metal case handcuffed to his wrist. He placed the case on a small chair to the side of the podium, unlocked his wrist, and affixed the handcuff to Alice's outstretched arm. Moss's breath caught as he watched with rapt anticipation.

"Now we enter a new epoch," Alice Carcer announced as the man excused himself from the stage. Even Benedict was quiet as his aunt spoke. "I am thrilled to announce that the Carcer Corporation has struck a new deal with NeoVerge Industries. Through a joint funding effort, we have established the first functional relay system in the universe: an intergalactic communication system unparalleled by anything seen before. Our employees will be able to speak with one another from distant planets as though they were standing together in a room.

"Why is this necessary, you ask? Well, you are the first to learn that NeoVerge, who run fifty-nine percent of the off-world colonies has hired Carcer to be their exclusive police force on every one of their colonies and everywhere in between."

The applause was so loud it shook the room, vibrating tables so hard the drinks spilled.

Moss could not believe what he was hearing. The company which had helped to make slaves of the citizens of earth was now primed to do the same thing everywhere where humans lived. They would become unstoppable, and Moss knew that they needed to steal that case. Even if it only worked for a short time before Carcer figured a way to shut it off, they needed to contact the free colonies and warn them of the impending chokehold Carcer would deliver.

Anders had spoken at length about the need to work with the off-worlders, and now they could have a way to do so.

Alice spoke over the ovation. "We have already begun recruitment for our new force, construction of a fleet, and soon, trade will resume between the planets unabated by the pirates and scoundrels who act as a scourge on our society!"

She banged her free hand on the podium, sending a ripple of sound through the already electrified room. "A secure universe is a safe universe, and the Carcer Corporation will bring that security to the stars just as it has to the earth!" she thundered as Moss's ears split at the deafening clamor.

"Shit," Moss murmured, the words falling silently from his

mouth amidst the racket. He had never thought his grand-mother smarter than he did in that moment. They needed to be here for this, needed to see with their own eyes the plans which Carcer had worked out with the AIC to take control of everything.

The room was electric with fever as Alice Carcer lifted one hand in salute and said, "Thank you and goodnight!"

The crowd did not settle down for a long time after she strode from the stage. All eyes turned to one another excitedly. People discussed business plans and ways they could capitalize on this new information.

"Pretty cool, eh?" Benedict said, turning to face Moss, his eyes wide with excitement.

Moss was hardly able to speak. "That's, something..."

"Man, I'm half-chubbed just from that speech. Let's go see if Molly can get me all the way there," Benedict suggested, turning Moss toward a side door.

He felt frozen, rooted to the spot. But he knew he needed to move.

He knew he needed that case.

CHAPTER 21

Benedict had sent his lackeys away and made Moss take another hit before proceeding. Moss hadn't had visions the second time as he had tried to steel his mind before snorting. The second hit struck his system like lighting, though, and he felt twitchy and in less control of himself than he wanted at a moment such as this.

"Think you can talk your way in?" Moss asked, hearing the nervousness in his voice.

Benedict turned wild eyes on him as they made their way to a staircase flanked on both sides by grim, angry-looking guards. "Oh, shit, yeah!" Benedict exclaimed. "Nothing's gonna stop me now!"

He strode up to the guards, his chest puffed up.

"We are going to visit security," he announced unwaveringly.

One of the guards scoffed. "Not a chance."

"Run back to your party, fancyboy," the other added. Unlike the guards at the entrance, these ones did not feel the need to kowtow to the guests.

Benedict laughed in their faces. "Do you have any idea who I am?"

The two guards looked him over. "You look like a couple of kids who are about to have their asses chucked into the street."

"With broken noses," the second intoned.

Benedict took a step closer in an attempt at intimidation. The guards did not flinch.

"You listen here, you fucking cows," he seethed. "I am Benedict Young, nephew of your boss's boss's boss's boss. I am the acting Senior Vice President of Global Talent Assessment at the company which signs your paychecks and likely successor to Carcer.

"Now, you may be telling yourself, 'We were given clear orders, and if we let them pass, we will lose our jobs,' but that is not how this chain of command works. Deny me one more time and you'll find out exactly the way the Carcer Corporation is run. Not only will you lose your jobs, but I'll put a bounty on you so high that your grandchildren's children will be sowing palmscreen nanomesh in a Rwandan sweatshop just to pay to house your corpses."

Moss couldn't believe what he was hearing. The way Benedict threatened these grunts was like nothing he had ever seen. Moss had hated the way he spoke to the man in the restroom, but watching it be inflicted upon Carcer operatives brought him a guilty joy.

The guards looked at one another.

"Sorry, sir," one said.

"Just trying to do our jobs, sir," the other added. "Please, just don't tell anyone."

Benedict smiled wickedly. "Don't try and give me another fucking order, and perhaps you won't be the first former employees to see the inside of the Ice Block."

"Yes, sir. My apologies, sir," the second guard said. "We will radio ahead to have them let you right in."

"Oh," Benedict snarled condescendingly, patting the huge man on the helmet. "You're learning."

Moss couldn't help but smile. Using a bad person as a weapon against bad people pleased him greatly.

They walked right past the guards and two more at the top of the stairs who simply nodded at them. They came to a heavy metal door, which beeped and unlocked when Benedict pounded a heavy fist.

Three technicians sat at a bank of screens showing every possible angle of the party, hallways, adjoining rooms, and surrounding streets. Moss looked to see if he could spot Gibbs hiding in one of the nearby buildings but was happy for his friend's sake that he could not.

Moss nodded toward a slender man in the corner, staring intently at an overview of the party floor. He had a beard of curly brown hair that attached to an unkempt mop on his head. Wire-rim glasses perched at the tip of a wide nose, leaving an indent in the flesh.

Benedict nodded and approached, tapping the man on the shoulder. As he swiveled in his chair to face them, Moss tried to plan his move. The technicians were all lightly armored and had sidearms holstered at their sides. He tried to see what model of weapon they carried but could not make it out, assuming they were the same Turaco brand pistols he had seen in Carcer City. If that was the case, Moss would need to make precise shots if he stood any chance of taking control of the room.

"What can I do for you, sir?" the man asked nervously, stopping to swallow between words.

"I just want you to show me something on here," Benedict said, the kind words not matching his hard tone.

"Yes, sir," the man said, nodding vigorously.

Benedict smiled. "These cameras have x-ray?"

The man looked like he was trying to hold back a smile at

Benedict's expense. "Well, it's not really x-ray, it's a form of. . ." but Benedict held up a hand.

"Not interested. Can you see through some bitches' clothes or not?" he hissed.

The man visibly trembled. "Yes, sir."

"Great," Benedict said, nearing the projected monitors. "Then zoom in here and let's see what she's working with."

The man said nothing by way of protest. He zoomed in on Molly as a digital flash enveloped the screen a moment before displaying the same image without the dress. Moss felt guilt and excitement in equal parts as he stared at the woman, holding her drink and chatting with a friend but shown completely nude. Moss couldn't help but take in her curves and the perfect shape of her body. His conscious mind knew this was invasive and disgusting, but the drugs had made him horny, and all thoughts of the mission took a backseat for a moment.

"How you don't do this all day, I'll never understand," Benedict said, patting the man on his thin shoulder. Benedict's other hand moved to stroke his engorging penis through his pant leg. Moss was dumbstruck by the young man's action. He couldn't believe that he would do something like that in public. It occurred to Moss that Benedict was likely so unaccustomed to limits or being told that he couldn't do something, that he felt comfortable treating the whole world as his personal playground.

The other two operators pretended to take no note of what they were doing, but it was obvious that they were taking side-long looks.

"You know Aya?" Benedict asked the man, and Moss hardly registered the name until the camera tilted and swayed to point at Ynna with another woman's face. Her perfect form standing nude amidst the party-goers snapped Moss back to reality.

Seeing his friend like that was vile, and he hated himself just before his eyes flashed down.

Quick as lightning, Moss's hand moved and flipped the clip on the man's weapon, loosing the pistol and pressing into his flank.

He pulled the trigger.

Once.

Twice.

The silent beams knocked the two men unconscious in a flash. The other operators turned, wide-eyed, as they reached for their own weapons. The one nearest Moss fumbled at his side as Moss pivoted and took the shot. The first hit the man's chest plate, dissipating into nothing, but the second struck him in the neck, sending him twirling in his chair before sliding to the ground.

The last operator was up and charged Moss. Moss pulled the trigger, but the battery connection failed, and the weapon flashed red just as Moss was speared to the ground. The air was knocked from his lungs as he crashed to the thin carpet.

He tried to raise the pistol, but she slammed his hand down. She was smart and well trained, and Moss knew he had to do one thing if he was going to survive this. He punched her hard in the throat so she couldn't call out.

She gasped for air while landing punches to Moss's face with her free hand. He felt the false skin pull against his own with each blow. They tussled around the floor until Moss managed to get one foot against her stomach.

With the force of his cybernetic leg, he pushed, and she careened across the room as if fired from a cannon. The sound of her hitting the wall was dull but shook the room slightly, and Moss blinked hard at the screens to see if more guards had been alerted.

He craned his neck with difficulty to see that no one was

rushing down any hallways. He worked hard to breathe, trying to calm himself.

A trickle of blood escaped the woman's mouth as she lay slumped in the corner, but he saw her hands move toward her weapon.

"No," he hissed at her. Her eyes were wild and angry, but her body was slow to react.

Moss pushed himself up to his feet, staggering over to her. He felt little pain but knew he had been hurt.

She pointed and shot wide, the bolt fizzling against the ceiling. Moss moved to her and snatched the weapon from her hand.

As he turned it on her, he gasped, "I'm sorry."

He didn't know what instinct made him say the words. He was only knocking her out, and he knew she would have killed him if given half a chance, but he still meant the apology.

He slumped into her chair, and it rolled halfway across the small room before he set his feet to stop it. Four people lay strewn about him as he slid over to the computers.

He now wished he had taken Ynna up on her offer. Within the program, things were easy, but looking at the security layout before him, he didn't know what he was doing. Taking slow, deep, difficult breaths, he took some time to familiarize himself with the layout.

He clicked through on the projected keyboard and found the root menu. He was faced with words he recognized but did not know the meaning of within this context and acronyms he tried to piece together. For a moment, he considered making his way back to the party and bringing Ynna up here before realizing how foolish an idea that was: Even if she wasn't needed to help steal the tech, there was no way he could make it beyond the layers of guards two more times without being found out—especially without Benedict.

He shut his eyes, wondering if his program could tap systems not controlled by ThutoCo.

His mind was in so many places at once that he didn't even get flashes of his hex and decided it was a waste of time anyway.

He clicked through to SECURITY PROTOCOLS and stared. It looked like nothing but a sea of letters. One caught his eye.

NND. He pressed it and another screen opened with a simple red ACTIVATE and green DEACTIVATE. He puzzled at the colors, thinking they should be the other way around before selecting DEACTIVATE.

Grandma? Ynna? he thought.

Well, no shit, he heard Sandra say in his mind.

How am I hearing you? Gibbs asked.

Your friend loves his control rooms, Ynna chided.

Anders cut in with a hurried tone, *Should I bring the ship around?*

Not yet, Moss told him.

Alright, kid, where is that queen bitch? Sandra asked.

Shit, give me a second, Moss said, realizing he should have found Alice's location before opening the network. He scanned square after square of images, his eyes darting between screens as he tried to find her. In the lower corner of one screen, he saw the woman. She was sitting in a side room with a few guests, talking and gesturing with the case still handcuffed to her wrist.

Moss traced the path to the room via several cameras mounted along the hallways, seeing layers of guards along the route. With a nervous hand, Moss snatched a radio off one of the limp bodies and put the headset on. He cleared his throat and depressed the communication button.

"This is Command to all units. Alice wishes to speak with Klasina Van Dijk. Please allow her and her daughter passage," Moss said, swallowing mid-sentence in an impression of the man who had operated the camera for them.

Moss watched the feed as the guards all listened to the command, and he heard in response, "Ten-four, command."

Moss's time playing a Carcer Officer back in the city was coming in handy. He leaned back in the chair, knowing that once he let them know, the real action would begin.

He sighed. *Alright, guys, you are cleared to meet with Alice Carcer through a door at the east side of the room. I'll keep eyes up here. Good luck.*

Moss watched as Ynna and Sandra converged on the party floor.

Good work, his grandmother told him, moving toward the door.

Just give the word, Anders said.

Moss moved to grab every weapon off all the guards and lay the pile on the desk in front of him.

Here we go, Ynna said, and the two women made their way to meet with Alice Carcer.

CHAPTER 22

Moss turned the volume up on the feed from Alice's small room. The guards opened the door from the other side and waved Sandra and Ynna in.

Alice looked up. "Klasina, Aya, welcome," she said with an ingratiating tone, but her face betrayed her surprise.

Sandra took her extended hand in one and placed the other on top. "Alice, a pleasure as always. Now, I know you weren't expecting us, but I wanted to come and congratulate you personally."

"You're too kind," Alice said. "And I'm thrilled you stopped by, truly. Feel free to enjoy the foods and the company of the other investors. I'm sure you know everyone here."

Sandra smiled wickedly in Klasina's face. "Actually," she said, pulling a gun from Ynna's purse and leveling it at Alice. "I think you and I will have a chat."

Alice's eyes registered surprise, but she wore a mask of calm self-assurance.

Ynna pressed a finger to her lips and gestured for all the terrified elite to sit where they were. Moss's heart pounded as he watched, terrified that someone might scream out. They all knew a firefight was inevitable but needed it to wait until they had the package and were on their way from the building. None of the people in the room said anything; they just lowered themselves to the floor in terror.

Alice did not sit, she simply leaned back against the table on which the case was set, stating at Sandra.

"I knew that I knew those eyes," she said with a smirk. "I watched *all* of the videos of you when you were our guest." She turned to Ynna. "I suppose that makes you Marina Hawkins?"

Ynna flushed as Alice turned back to Sandra. "And I'm guessing your grandson and his plump friend are right outside this door. You're a brazen woman, I'll grant you that, but you have overreached too far this time."

"We'll see about that," Sandra snarled.

Alice nodded. "Indeed, we will. You have invaded a fortress with, what, half a dozen untrained children? I have an army. Here, and everywhere around here. For fuck's sake, I run the largest army in the world. You'll die today. She'll die today and so will your only family."

Sandra was simply smiling, letting the woman speak, but Moss felt the words. They had an exit strategy and escape plan. They had done something impossible already: infiltrating this party. But hearing Alice Carcer's threats, Moss was petrified. He wondered if they *had* overreached.

With one eye on the screen, he began to look back at the security controls. Seeing all the guards on all the screens distracted him and he swallowed hard. He began trying to see if he could take control of the machine gun turrets throughout the building as his grandmother finally spoke.

"You may have an army and this building, but we have the people of this world. You are an agent of evil who is working with the AIC to move your enslavement of this world to all the others," she said quietly, her voice threatening as she moved closer to Alice. "We will expose you all for what you are, and the people will rise up to tear you down."

Alice Carcer let out a genuine laugh. "You are more naïve than I even thought."

"What, you're going to deny the existence of the AIC, now?" Sandra snorted.

"Oh, no, it's just you misunderstand our goals," she chuckled. "We have no interest in enslaving the people of this planet."

"Now, who's being naïve. You think I believe that?" Sandra scoffed. Ynna continued to point her weapon menacingly at the cowering guests.

Alice shook her head. "It doesn't matter what you believe."

She smiled broadly.

Moss saw a massive alert cross all the screens.

He reached out.

DEACTIVATE.

She initiated a panic sequence, Moss informed them. *I turned it off.*

Alice's eyes darted a moment before Sandra let forth a small laugh of her own. "You ain't so clever as you think."

For the first time, Moss saw fear cross the stern woman's face.

"You say we are surrounded, and you have an army and all that," Sandra told her. "But we ain't so foolish. We got to you when you thought you were safe, and now we are going to take that new toy of yours right out from under your nose."

"*This* is what you want?" Alice asked in disbelief.

Sandra nodded.

Alice continued to look at her with shock. "It's propriety Carcer tech. You'll never be able to access it."

"We will," Sandra told her. "We always do."

Alice shifted slightly to put her hand on the box, the chain rattling against the metal. "Also," and she looked around the room. "It isn't ready yet. The relays are just going up now. We were using tonight to drum up interest in investment."

Moss's heart sank. He had known at ThutoCo that many companies would fake innovations until they secured the funds to actually produce them. Mr. Greene had always joked that it was "as foolish a practice as it was common."

If the technology wasn't actually ready, this whole venture would be for nothing.

"I don't buy what you're selling," Sandra said. "I know it'll work."

Moss expected Alice to give another snarky answer, but the woman seemed vexed, trying to think of the next thing she could say to keep the technology.

"Plus," Sandra said, leaving an ominous pause in her words. "It's only part of the reason we are here."

Moss and Alice knew the truth at the same moment, and Ynna turned to look at Sandra.

"No," Ynna implored and Moss felt his stomach turn.

Sandra hissed over her shoulder, "You keep quiet."

With Sandra distracted for a moment, and realizing how desperate her situation had become, Alice lifted the box and swung it toward Sandra. The case struck her in the shoulder, causing her to fall. The case carried Alice to the ground as well. "Help me!" she called to the guests, two of whom rushed toward Ynna.

She fired once, killing one attacker instantly, but the other knocked her to the ground and attempted to wrestle the weapon free.

Moss saw that the two guards on the other side of the door heard the commotion. Moss pressed the locking mechanism on the screen and secured them inside.

Get that ship ready, Anders. he commanded. *Gibbs, be on alert.*

The guards began to bang on the door, and Moss heard radio

chatter fill the headset. Men and women began to pour toward the room and, to his horror, the control room as well.

He locked himself in and tried again to take control of the turrets. The same override screen appeared, and no password he entered did anything.

He watched as Sandra and Alice staggered to their feet. Sandra turned her pistol at the man grabbing Ynna and shot him in the back, blood spraying the room. She had obviously taken the weapon with more stopping power.

Alice tried to lift the box with both hands so she could move more easily, but her wrist had been damaged trying to throw the case. Sandra held the weapon aloft.

"No more heroics," Ynna told the remaining guests.

"Fine, take it," Alice panted. "See how far you get."

Without saying a word, Sandra moved faster than Moss had ever seen. She pulled the ceremonial blade from Alice's side and with lightning speed, sliced it through her wrists. The case fell to the floor in a shower of crimson. The person who controlled the world's largest army screamed. The little white dog, who had faithfully followed the two, whimpered.

Alice fell to her knees as Sandra put a heeled shoe into the blood and slid the case toward Ynna.

Moss heard a pounding on the door outside. He turned before looking back toward the pile of weapons arrayed in front of him.

He sighed. Seeing the screen, he counted more guards than he could survive.

His eyes moved with somber desperation to his grandmother. She wasn't supposed to cut off her hands. Alice Carcer was supposed to be their bargaining chip, but bleeding out, she would be useless. Her death would mean their certain demise. Moss hoped that she would survive long enough to get them out.

"You fucking lunatic," Alice sputtered, her color draining from her flesh. Her normally bright eyes now lost, sunk deep into an increasingly skeletal face. Sandra moved forward and pressed the barrel against her forehead.

"We need her," Ynna pleaded. "You can kill her after, later."

"No," Sandra said, and Moss felt his heart sink.

This had always been a vendetta.

His grandmother had spent so long in that prison, being tortured and abused. Moss knew that she had wanted to do good and see this mission through, but now he understood how truly damaged she had become.

He had missed it with Irene and had been able to stop Puck, but now he felt hopeless.

Grandma, he pleaded. *We need her.*

She tilted her head toward the camera mounted in the corner of the room. *No, Moss, we don't.*

"Do it!" he heard Arthur Smith shout in his head as he watched his grandmother pull the trigger.

"No!" he shouted aloud as Alice Carcer's head blew backward.

MOSS SAW WHITE.

He blinked and he knew.

She had known. That drunken night, Moss had told his grandmother that his emotions had once unlocked the program. She must have been banking on that.

"Some good it will do," Moss said. "Unless. . ." and it dawned on him that she may have also known more than she had let on.

He moved to his console and saw all the same Carcer screens that he had seen before in the control room. He watched as the guards leveled their weapons at the door while others moved into positions around the building and still more hurried down the streets.

In that moment, he didn't care that she had kept him in the dark once again or how he was able to hack more than just ThutoCo. He was just grateful that he could.

He brought up the security defense system and opened the menu for the turrets.

There was no encryption, no passwords, nothing. Somehow, somewhere, the program was breaking the system itself. Moss realized just how much of a genius his mother had truly been.

He watched as his mind began targeting the guards. One after another, the system tracked them. Throughout the building, boxes appeared over their bodies and flashed green.

Moss couldn't believe what he was able to do, or what he was about to do.

All at once, the screens lit up with muzzle flash. Bodies fell everywhere as the building was painted in blood.

He saw his grandmother grin at the sound of it as she scooped up the case.

He unlocked the doors before them, and he watched as they climbed over the bodies to begin their escape.

On one screen, he looked to the control room to his own body which was lying slumped on the ground. All that he was doing in his mind was exhausting his physical form. He knew he needed to escape, but also that he couldn't leave the program yet.

Need some help here, Anders called out, and Moss looked to the roof of the building. Guards were rushing about, pulling themselves into anti-aircraft guns, and taking potshots at the dropship. Gibbs was picking them off slowly, but he couldn't do it alone.

Moss opened another menu to take control of one of the AA

guns but looked back to his body on the ground. He couldn't protect the ship and escape.

He could sacrifice himself but knew that, unlike at Carcer City, he would not survive this.

A thought occurred to him. He didn't know if it could work but had to try.

"Two," he said, reaching into the program with his mind.

"Didn't expect to hear from you so soon," the AI joked.

"I need you to do something," Moss told it.

The computer chuckled. "I already blocked transmission of this communication, but, you know, I did it *before* ThutoCo was alerted this time."

Moss nodded. "Thanks, but that's not what I meant."

"I'm going to try something radical," he said, selecting an upload menu and dragging the icon toward his body on the screen.

"What's that?" Two asked.

"I need you to get my body to the roof of this building while I stay in this program and fend off some assholes."

The computer laughed again. "Alright, here we go."

Moss selected his body and uploaded the AI to control the chip.

He watched his fingers twitch.

His body stood.

"Whoa," Two said and the world went quiet for just a moment as he realized that a computer was controlling his physical body while his consciousness was controlling a computer program. "I'm a real boy," Moss heard Two joke in his mind's ear.

Seriously, Anders shouted, and the moment passed. He had to focus.

Moss selected an automated turret on the roof and tilted the twin cannons down, spraying heavy fire at the other weapons on the roof. Smoke billowed into the sky as the world was alight with bullets and shells. Metal exploded and guards screamed in confusion as they turned to shoot the rogue turret.

Moss continued the volley as he watched the ship move to land on the roof. Gibbs fired up his dronepack and began to fly over the street as Ynna and Sandra ascended one staircase, and Moss's body, another.

As his body rounded a corner, a remaining guard raised an autorifle. With machine efficiency, Moss's arms moved to pull the weapon free and turned it to spray the guard with bullets. Moss was amazed at what Two was able to do when controlling a human body. He worried, just for a moment, if ThutoCo had considered this.

Sandra and Ynna burst onto the flaming roof, stepping over steaming metal and body parts. Smoke curled outward as the ship moved to land, the thrusters adding more heat and fumes to the chaotic scene.

"Alright, Two, I'm coming back," Moss said, and he shut his eyes as his body made its way toward the ship.

PEACE WASHED over Moss as he opened his eyes, but the feeling passed in an instant. He gagged on the smoke and remembered the drugs and the beating he had taken. It was the most bizarre sensation he had ever felt, the literal out-of-body experience ending abruptly as his mind took control of his body. He felt pain everywhere, and it was not easy to move. His steps faltered and Gibbs reached out, pulling Moss into the ship as it began to lift slowly into the night sky.

"I knew you could do it," Sandra said as Moss fell into one of the seats, panting and blinking hard to regain his focus. His grandmother was picking pieces of her false face off her wrinkled skin before making her way across the tight space and hugging him. His eyes welled as he pulled her close. He had more questions than ever about the nature of reality, his mind, and the program, but they all washed away in her embrace.

"*We* did do it," Moss croaked as he looked at the case. They had successfully stolen technology which could help them save both this world and the ones beyond. They had killed Alice Carcer, a blight on the earth. They had done it all together. Moss, his friends, and his parents, whose legacy of fighting for right lived within him.

He knew that they would be hunted with more ferocity than ever now and that things would be more difficult than ever before, but in that moment, he didn't care.

He looked around the ship at the people he loved. "Let's go home."

THE END

EPILOGUE

A rthur Smith felt good. Dressed all in black, the President of ThutoCo was happier than he had been in a long time. Alice Carcer had been a constant thorn in his side since he had invited her to join the Amalgamated Interests Council. She had agreed to work toward their common goal, but he had always known that she was making side deals and backroom agreements to further her interests more than the Council's.

Hearing of her deal with NeoVerge Industries, which he learned from his mole inside her gala, had only intensified this belief. Now, she was dead. Killed by rogue agents who, while they were led by a former employee of his, couldn't actually be traced back to him. It was a boon.

The Carcer Corporation was a notoriously poorly run company whose board would appoint some lackey to run things in her stead. Arthur knew he could manipulate this new person with ease and could get the AIC back on track.

He would vie to take his role back at its head, and with Carcer's recent black eye, no one would fight it.

He smiled as he strode toward the door to the conference room on the top floor of The Idyllic Tower—ThutoCo's headquarters in BA City. The company's founder had been obsessed with (among many things) the city's early history and constructed a building gilded in gold to honor the early pioneers of western expansion. While most of the citizenry now regarded it as a monument to corporate oppression, Arthur regarded the building as a testament to the power of single-minded vision and drive.

He turned his face into a severe frown befitting the mood before walking into the room. A long, rectangular Dahlbergian wood table was set with pitchers of unprocessed water taken directly from a source in the Alps, recently steeped tea hand-picked in protected fields in China, and pots of fresh coffee grown in former Ethiopia and roasted in Italy. Metal and crystal lights styled to look like tree branches grew from two holes in the ceiling. Original Katsushika Hokusai prints hung on the wall, though everyone in the room ignored them. Arthur liked to furnish spaces with things he could admire, preferring form over function in his aesthetic.

The AIC had only met in person once before, at its genesis. The group comprised mostly of older men sitting quietly, sipping drinks, and working remotely on palmscreens.

The door opened automatically, and Arthur entered to somber nods of greeting. Samir Balwani shot daggers at him as he sat at the head of the table.

"Sorry, Sam," Arthur said, playing at kindness despite their mutual mistrust.

The President of NeoVerge Industries, who had come to Earth for the funeral, gave Arthur a somber look. "Condolences to you as well. I know you two were close," he said, sounding sincere. Arthur nodded, knowing that all the people in the room could lie as easily and naturally as breathe.

"Any word on recovering your technology? The system

sounded cutting edge, and I'm hoping to work with you on it moving forward," Arthur told him.

Samir flinched but regained his composure in an instant. "We have people trying to track down *your* employee and should have it back in our possession in no time."

"I certainly hope so," Arthur lied. "It was a bold move letting her take it for the presentation."

"It didn't feel like it at the time as we were still in Series B funding, but Alice paid for our error far more than I did," Samir said, pinching the edge of his beard between thumb and forefinger. He was a wiry man, far more fit than most in the room, and he wore a suit of fine Indian materials, though it was said he had never visited the country of his ancestors.

"She did," Arthur agreed, masking his jubilance.

"What she did," Derek Sterling introjected from across the table, "was die for your fucking plan, Artie."

Arthur cringed as the murmuring in the room fell silent.

He hated Derek. Hated the nicknames, the casual attire he always wore, the body odor, and more than anything, the stranglehold that D2E had on all of Earth's entertainment.

With a grimace, Arthur turned to face the room. "My plan... *our* plan is a good one and one which will make every person in this room rich beyond our wildest dreams."

The dubious looks made him hyper-aware that he needed to work hard to regain their faith. "We are being stifled and held back by our current limitations. If we continue on the path I have laid out, our accomplishment will be remembered in the annals of history.

"Sure, we *have* suffered some setbacks," he said but was cut short by Derek guffawing theatrically.

"Some setbacks!?" he chortled. "That fucking kid, his grandma, and, like, six children are making you—or rather—all of us look like a bunch of clowns. I'm trying to sway the narrative for you, but people are paying attention. You wouldn't believe the clickthrough rate of stories about them! If you want our continued cooperation, we are all going to need to know that this shit is being handled."

Everyone in the room nodded in agreement. Arthur swallowed hard. This was not going how he had planned. He had hoped that Alice's death would have reinvigorated the group to work together, but not against him.

He cleared his throat. "I know that these few terrorists have been a problem, but I plan to have them dealt with in short order. Rumor has it that they are back in BA and we should have no trouble in eliminating them."

"We have heard that before," Zhang Wei, head of Xuefeng Technologies, said bluntly. The room erupted into comments and questions, and Arthur knew he was losing them.

He shouted, "We also plan to work with Carcer to—" but he was cut off once again as the doors to the room swung open violently. An olive-skinned man with a dark mustache, even darker eyes, and full Carcer armor strode into the room.

"Work with us to do what?" he sneered.

"This is a private meeting," Arthur announced.

The man smiled wickedly, placing his hands on his hips and turning a withering gaze on Arthur. "I was invited," he snorted.

Caught off guard, Arthur simply muttered, "What?"

"Alice Carcer was no fool," he said in a commanding tone that seemed to fill every millimeter of the room. "In the event of her untimely demise, I would be appointed Interim Dictator of Carcer Corporation."

"And just who the hell are you and why should we care?" Derek asked, putting saddle clad feet on the table. While Arthur was mortified by this revelation, Derek seemed wholly unimpressed.

"I am Warden Ninety-Nine," he thundered. "The only man

who has twice captured the terrorist Moss. And why you should care is because I will do so again. I will reclaim control of the planet that Mister Smith has lost and when I do, I will turn my attention to those who have aided him."

He looked squarely at Arthur. "The people in this room may not be aware that it was corporate agents who freed the terrorist in Cape City."

At this, the murmuring began again. "And as such," Ninety-Nine continued, "we will have to re-evaluate the role of the AIC and our involvement in it."

The wealthiest and most powerful people on the planet all turned to speak to one another, and Arthur knew that all he had worked for was beginning to slip away. He wracked his brain for something to say but the large man leaned right into his face. "We know you freed the kid, and I suspect you funded his attack on our facility. Once I kill Moss and all his little friends, I *will* avenge Alice."

NOTE TO THE READER

Thanks for reading Digital Walls: A Cyberpunk Saga (Book 3). If you enjoyed the book, please leave a review, it is incredibly helpful to authors. Reviews are one of the ways in which people can discover new work and help me to create more of it. I read all the reviews and love to hear what people think of my work. Thanks again for reading.

For more information and bonus content, visit Thuto-World.com

AUTHOR BIO

Matthew A. Goodwin has been writing about spaceships, dragons, and adventures since he was twelve years old. His passion for fantasy began when he discovered a boxed set of the Hobbit radio drama on cassette tape in his school's library at the age of seven. He fell in love with fantasy worlds and soon discovered D&D and Warhammer miniatures.

Not wanting to be limited by worlds designed by others, he created Thutopia (now called the Thuton Empire), a fantasy world of his own that he still writes about to this day.

Like many kids with an affinity for fantasy, a love of science fiction soon followed. He loved sweeping space operas and gritty cyberpunk stories that asked questions about man's relationship to technology. That led him to write his first published work, Into Neon: A Cyberpunk Saga, which takes place in a larger science fiction universe.

He has a passion for travel and wildlife, and when he is not off trying to see the world, he lives in San Francisco with his wife and son.

Made in the USA
Las Vegas, NV
27 November 2022

60446252R00163